Shark ...ing in Paradise Garden

Cameron Pierce

Eraserhead Press
Portland, OR

ERASERHEAD PRESS

205 NE BRYANT
PORTLAND, OR 97211

WWW.ERASERHEADPRESS.COM

ISBN: 1-933929-77-4

For Tanuki

"All paradises are artificial."

-Louis Aragon

"So was it with the evil seed of Adam; They threw themselves from that shore one by one, As they were beckoned, like birds obeying a call."

-Dante's Inferno, Canto III

CHAPTER ONE
After the Crash

My silk bathrobe drips blood and gold.

I peel a still-beating leprechaun heart from my forehead and pull myself up by the cracked glass of my egg-shaped incubator. Inside the Gibarian, it's golden arteries and icicles of coagulated blood, leprechauns impaled on spidery machines, and at least three dozen priests leaky and limbless in their own bathrobes. I sift through a cave of fried wiring and leprechaun flesh and there lies Zelda, my wife and second-in-command of Yahweh's Dawn, her bathrobe ripped and scattered around her body. What remains of her vagina is a ring of bite marks circling a chewed two-foot rope of clitoris like an eyeless smiley face sticking out its tongue. The things that ate the limbs of the other priests spared Zelda's arms. For this, I am almost thankful.

I kneel beside her and cross her hands across her breasts. "I can't bury you right now, but I promise to come back. Hang tight, babe. Adam and Eve will know what to do." I mumble a quick prayer and turn away from Zelda's corpse to stagger toward the Gibarian's emergency exit.

I reach out to open the trilunium door and notice Kelvin's black top hat. Just over three feet tall, Kelvin had been the tallest leprechaun. He's probably in a billion pieces now. He won't need his top hat anymore. I reach down and pick it up. Zelda always liked when I wore a top hat.

3

I suck in a breath of air and open the door. This might be the last second of my life.

A black sun and chartreuse sky blind me. I lower the top hat to shield my eyes and squint at the turtle shell trees surrounding the ship in every direction. The leaves quiver and chirp. They aren't leaves at all, but crickets.

Ancestor patrols the edge of the clearing where the Gibarian crashed. He twirls his battle axe in his gorilla hands. A bundle of bamboo spears dangles from his crocodile jaws. I hop down from the exit door and wave to him. It's good to know that even if Zelda has abandoned me for God, someone still exists to die here in Paradise Garden. No one gets out of here alive, not without a time machine, and ours seems to be fucked beyond repair.

"Where the hell have you been?" Ira shouts.

I spin around. She stands among a few other priests about twenty yards away. As I approach, Sturgeonwolf pats my shoulder with one of his sturgeon growths. I ignore him. He is the only priest I never liked, mostly because he's a lazy halfwit whose interpretations of the Jheronimus, the main text of Yahweh's Dawn, reflect absolutely nothing our sect believes in. Sturgeonwolf stumbles off to bother Ancestor and I ask the others how we crashed. More importantly, who killed Zelda and the leprechauns?

Wayne, an armless wizard head and high priest of Yahweh's Dawn, stumbles up to me on his fat lizard legs. "A shark attacked the Gibarian before we entered Paradise Garden's atmosphere, somewhere beyond the hyperspace jungle. Over eighty percent of the crew has been confirmed deceased, among them Zelda and Bergstrom. My condolences about Zelda."

Ira squeezes her razor-edged Jerry (short for Jheronimus) until her knuckles whiten. She shoots me one of her superbitch glares that make me think she's demon-possessed. Her spiky-dark hair glares at me and for all I know, every part of Ira must be in need of an exorcism right now. "Why did you bring them along?" she says.

"Who?" I say, playing dumb so I can pretend not to hear what Wayne has said. I'd rather have cancer than condolences.

"You know who," Ira says, raising her Jerry.

Wayne steps between us. "Ernest is right," he says. "We needed the leprechauns. They're good luck, and Eve wrote that she was interested in breeding them here. If Anton secured his passengers. . . ."

Rattlesnake Doctor looks up from stitching a gaping cut on Donkey's arm and exhales a loud hiss. Anton strolls over and lifts Wayne by his white beard. "Those freaks weren't my passengers," Anton says, his rubber bird beak poking Wayne in the face.

Anton is another priest I don't give much of a damn about. That's not to say I dislike him, just that he's a lousy pilot.

Wayne's legs dangle in the air like toothpicks stuck in Vienna Sausages. He babbles something about feathers and flesh-eating umbrellas.

"Don't cast one of your spells on me," Anton says.

"Watch out. He's going to turn your feathers into flesh-eating umbrellas," I warn Anton.

Ira shoves me aside. She snatches Wayne from Anton's grip just as Ancestor approaches. Sturgeonwolf shuffles behind him. Ancestor takes the bamboo spears from his mouth and says, "We should get as far from here as possible before dark. Sharks will swarm the wreckage soon."

Rattlesnake Doctor wipes blood from his snakeskin

boots and vest. Along with Donkey, the Doctor refuses to wear our traditional silk bathrobes. He swigs from a jar of venom and wipes his mouth on the back of a diamond-patterned hand and then returns to stitching Donkey's arm. As the needle slides through the pale flab of his arm, Donkey hee-haws and pounds the side of his rusted Spanish knight's helmet with his free fist.

"Those bleeding should stay," Ancestor says. "Our robes as well. Sharks will smell the blood."

"It isn't your decision to leave the wounded behind," Rattlesnake Doctor hisses.

"They're putting us all at risk," Ancestor says.

Donkey whimpers. "Don't leave me behind," he says. "I promise not to bleed anymore."

Wayne slaps his wooden twig tail against the blue-hazy dirt. "As founder of Yahweh's Dawn and director of this expedition, I say no one remains behind. We've lost too many priests as it is, and we can't leave the robes. Without them, Adam and Eve won't believe it's us. The scanners in our robes might be the only form of identification that didn't burn in the crash."

Anton squawks and flaps his hand-wings.

"Fine," Ancestor says. He shoves his bamboo spears between his teeth and marches away.

I hate when things get like this, everyone arguing and leaving me with nothing to say. It reminds me of all the times before joining Yahweh's Dawn when Zelda argued with me so loud the neighbors called the cops. When we joined Yahweh's Dawn, I looked forward to escaping the senseless nuthouse of each other. I discovered long ago that I was wrong. Zelda was crazy.

Anyway, because of an incurable disease doctors call pataphytitis, I possess two abilities: One, I can transform

6

into a toadman, and two, I can transform other things into mannequin versions of themselves. It's not as good as being Jesus and making lots of bread appear, but I'm incapable of pulling off more impressive magic. The tricks used to distract Zelda from burning me with hot fireplace pokers and using me as an archery target, at least some of the time, and sometimes the tricks distract the other priests from arguing. So I perform both at once. I morph into my amphibian self and hop around, turning cricket trees into mannequin trees.

I transform about a dozen trees into mannequins and then glance back at the group. Only Wayne notices me. He gives me a sad wizard frown. Wayne depresses me. Between all the wizard garbage and the awkward way his tiny legs support his big head, he could have walked right out of a bad fantasy novel. The others argue about our robes and where Adam and Eve live from here and whose fault it is that almost everyone died. Ira suggests that we're not in Paradise Garden at all, but in Hell. "Look at all the bugs," she says, indicating the trees.

It makes no sense for us to be in Hell because we devote our lives to God and the Jerry. We live for the Word. We are not eligible for Hell. But maybe Ira's onto something when she says she regrets that Adam and Eve ever invited us to Paradise Garden for a week of shark hunting. Hunting is a waste of time.

I search for something that might be more exciting as a mannequin. The trees don't seem to cut it for the others. The black sun falls lower and the greenedelic sky darkens to a swampy shade.

Kicking my feet into the blue dirt, a rainbow tail emerges and then burrows into the dirt again. I fall to my knees and dig with my toad hands. The slimy tail thrashes as I grab it with my fingers. I dig and claw and pull the entire

7

creature from the dirt. It has a trout's tail and a trout's body. The head is a yellow slug bearing decayed fangs. It squirms in my hands but I'm careful to avoid its jaws. Since we've seen no living animals in Paradise Garden, unless the cricket trees count, I want to show the others before turning this one into a mannequin.

The slug trout swivels its head. I panic about those teeth and squeeze too hard, transforming the slug trout into a mannequin. I'm bummed and disappointed, but holding a strange new creature that might distract the others.

"Check it out," I say, hopping over to them.

They step closer to see what I've got. "What the hell is that? Another one of your puppets?" Ira says.

"Is it dangerous?" Ancestor says, reaching for his battleaxe.

"It's a Dracula Slugfish. That's what my wizard senses tell me," Wayne says.

We all agree that it must be a Dracula Slugfish and then they yell at me for turning it into a mannequin and not being serious enough to make myself useful. Donkey says that maybe Dracula Slugfish and not sharks attacked the Gibarian.

"You're such a pathetic idiot," Ira says. I think she's talking to Donkey, but she stares directly at me. "A fucking disgrace," she says.

Ancestor shakes his head. "Had to be sharks. We've got to move or they'll be on us soon. Besides, Adam and Eve have no way of knowing we crashed."

The sun sinks below the horizon. I return to human form. This happens automatically at dusk. My stomach grumbles. None of us have eaten since leaving Earth, if we even left Earth. Travel through hyperspace, or time travel, remains controversial despite being relatively commonplace.

A school of thinkers known as the Right Time Consortium, although riddled with quacks and conspiracy freaks, believe that time travelers never leave the planet and are in fact only injected further inside the Great Outer Dream.

The RTC are all a bunch of mind terrorists who brainwashed the government into funding their cause. Yahweh's Dawn keeps as far from them as possible. We also avoid the anti-RTC camp, which the robot party overtook around the same time the Right Time Consortium rose to power. Since religious sects are legally recognized as a religion only if they support one party or the other, most people view Yahweh's Dawn as a cult of transsexual hippie bikers, since that's how a popular webshow host described us last year. None of our members are (or were) hippies or bikers, and both transsexuals are dead.

"Listen," Wayne says, "I want Ancestor, Anton, and Sturgeonwolf to patrol the area for enemies. Everyone else can salvage supplies from the Gibarian. There might be some food and weapons remaining. Rattlesnake Doctor, ensure that Donkey's arm is clean. No one gets left behind."

"Hold on a minute," Ira says, "you're saying you plan on tromping through this forest tonight?"

"There isn't time," Ancestor says.

Ira mutters another *fucking disgrace* and tucks her razor-edged Jerry under her arm. She walks away and disappears between a cluster of mannequin trees. I stare at the Dracula Slugfish in my hands and consider chucking it in her direction. Sturgeonwolf calls after her but she says nothing and never returns. Anton calls out too, and then we all do. The sky darkens from swamp-colored to nothing-colored and unless we're going to lose Ira forever, we see no choice but to follow.

CHAPTER TWO
First Night in Paradise

As we trek through our first night in Paradise, the leaves of the cricket trees chirp and hop among the tooth-like bark of the turtle shell trunks. Each time a cricket leaf jumps to a different turtle trunk, it instantly reattaches itself. Anton is the first to spot the Dracula Slugfish slithering up the trees. He squawks as the slugfish chomp down on the living leaves. The glowing heads of the slugfish provide our only light and there can't be more than a few dozen of them.

"It's Paradise Garden's version of bats and insects," Donkey says, always the astute fucking biologist.

Were they bats, I might be the one squawking and squealing. Flying rodents scare me shitless. Fortunately, we've encountered nothing in this part of Paradise Garden except Dracula Slugfish and cricket trees. Even if bats live here, I guess we might not be so bad off. Blood cakes our robes and bats hate red bathrobes.

Rattlesnake Doctor flicks his tongue. Since Ira stormed away from the crash site, he blames her for getting us so lost. I secretly blame her as well, but Ira might kick my ass if I say so. I'm a weakling except for my mannequin power, and the others would sacrifice me to God if I transformed any one of us into a mannequin. It's the same as murder to them. Ira is a bully and an emotional vampire. She also enjoys pointing out flaws in other people when someone blames her for anything. "If you flick your fucking tongue one more time, I'm going to cut if off," she says to the Doctor. "It's such an ugly tongue."

"No one is removing any tongues tonight," Wayne says.

Ancestor remains in the lead, on guard. "Sharks," he says. "There must be sharks around here."

"It's too dark for goddamn sharks," I say.

"Never use the Lord's name in vain," Wayne scolds.

I flip him off. He's walking in front of me and doesn't know. I say, "If you all came here to bitch and moan, you should have stayed at the monastery. All I want to do is meet up with Adam and Eve and do some hunting."

"I thought you told me you didn't like to hunt," Ira says.

When Ira traps you and you know it, ignoring her is the best policy. Ignoring people is usually the best policy. They act less lousy when you ignore them.

Ira kicks me in the ass from behind. "Tell me, Ernest," she says, "can you even name the Thirteen Commandments? I'd love to hear them, you cynical shit."

Ancestor grunts. He might be a lame ass priest, but he's the only true warrior among us. Ten years ago, a group of Japanese scientists conducted a study on immortality and discovered that Ancestor is almost impossible to kill. After they released the results, some huge supplement company contacted him about creating a product from his DNA. These days, everyone who's anyone in cage fighting begins using Ancestor-XL by age ten. It's actually Ancestor's royalties and subsequent sponsorships that provide most of our income. Otherwise, we'd have kicked him out years ago. His bad attitude disgraces the priesthood.

"Fucking Adam and Eve," I say, kicking dirt onto

Wayne, "leaving us stranded like this. I mean, what rude asses."

"They didn't strand us," Wayne says.

Sturgeonwolf chimes in with a *that's right.*

Ancestor halts and lunges toward me. He swings his battleaxe above my head, the same battleaxe which he made from the bones of his father after they fought to the death. He swings again and chops down three cricket trees in one swift motion. Obviously he doesn't get my joke.

He lowers his jaws to my ear and wheezes vinegar-frothy crocodile breath in my face. "Shutup or beat it," he says.

Too petrified to speak and mortified that I, of all people, pissed him off, I crack a smile.

"The more we walk, the less I understand why we came," Donkey says, his tumor-hump hunched over more than ever.

Wayne coughs. I can tell Donkey's remark hurts him. "We came because Adam and Eve invited us. It's about time Yahweh's Dawn gets the recognition it deserves. I've waited my entire life for an opportunity to visit Paradise Garden, although I must say, this hike reminds me of a winter I spent boxing in an underground Alaskan organization."

"You have no arms to box with," Ira says.

"Of course not," Wayne says, "because that slimy bastard Cthulhu bit them off in the championship bout. I'm sure you've heard the name Cthulhu, haven't you? Without arms, they forced me to retire. Ernest knows all about this. Just ask him."

The others look to me to verify and continue the story. Of course I've heard of Cthulhu. She's the heavyweight cage fighting champion of the world and the first fighter to attribute her success to Ancestor-XL. As for this Alaskan boxing league, Wayne must be getting senile, or else he's constipated. I notice he exaggerates a lot when he's constipated, and also when he feels inadequate. Maybe that's it. He's threatened because Ancestor keeps asserting his physical superiority. Wayne always has some bullshit experience to counter everyone's true experiences. When I first met him, he told me about his then-recent attempt to become a crab fisherman. He failed miserably and since I had failed at being a street magician around the same time, we pitied our failures together and became good friends. It turns out that what he meant when he said he failed at crab fishing is that he couldn't buy a train ticket out of Nebraska so that he might find a crab fishing job in the Pacific Northwest. I've come to ignore his tall tales.

"This isn't any place a knight can call a home," Donkey says, removing the group's attention from me. He raps his knuckles on his fourteenth century breastplate.

Wayne says, "I'd like to be sitting by a fire in Adam and Eve's cottage as much as you, Donkey, but that's—"

Donkey tackles Wayne and slaps his cheeks with an open hand. "I am not a Donkey. I am the Don of Keys. If none of you can respect me, I can't be a part of this anymore."

Ira, mocking Donkey's lethargic Barney Rubble voice, says, "He's the Don of Keys, the greatest Spanish knight there ever was. Be kind or he won't be your friend."

"The Don of Keys is right," I say. "We've got to respect each other to stick together. It's too lonely without you guys."

"Oh, come on," Ira says. "Your wife just died and you could give a flying fuck. In all my life, I've never met such an insensitive, disrespectful prick as you. Who are you to talk about respect and loneliness? I hope you're lonely. More than that, I hope you die lonely and that God—"

"Enough," Ancestor shouts. He pulls Donkey off of Wayne.

Ira shuts her trap and then Sturgeonwolf opens his. "Look! There are lights ahead," he says, all the while flapping his sturgeon growths.

Ancestor slips his battleaxe into the non-leather holster on his right hip. He pulls his bamboo spears from the sheath attached to his back and raises a spear to eye level, clamping down on the other spears in his jaws.

Wayne, Donkey, Anton, and Rattlesnake Doctor shuffle behind Ancestor while the rest of us guard the rear. "This could be an ambush," Rattlesnake Doctor says. He falls back from the others and steps along beside me. We're probably the most suited to ensure that nothing sneaks up on us.

As we approach, the red lights ghoul-flutter like sea anemones or bloody noses. With all the trees and the smothering soup of night, I haven't adjusted very well to the darkness. Discerning distance is not my strong point. Maybe those twenty yards are actually ninety . . . or one.

We stumble upon a circle of lights. They turn out to be squid growing from the dirt like flowers. A rose juts from the belly of every squid. Each rose waves ten feet in the air. Whenever two squid-flowers touch, they jerk back as if appalled by the prospect of other life. The squid part of the plant pulses shades of red and lightens to pork pink at the tips of the rose petals.

I approach one of the plants and poke the squid part with my index finger. The animal-plant flakes at the touch. I poke the same squid again and again, then rub it all over until the rose falls off the stalk and slithers away into the dark forest. Red slime fizzes where the squid used to be, then it reshapes itself in squid form. Almost as soon as the squid roots itself in the soil, a new rose grows.

The other priests inch closer as I kill the squid-flower again. It pisses me off when bugs refuse to die, and this one stinks like mildewed fish.

Starving and tired, I decide to risk eating a squid-flower. I grab the squid part and pull it from the soil. A faint electric jolt pulses through my hands as the outer flesh of the creature disintegrates.

Ira stands over me. "What the hell are you doing?" she says. Her breath feels hot against my neck. I wonder if one of her she-devil shrieks is on its way.

Ancestor shakes his crocodile jaws back and forth. He says, "Just to warn you, if that flower blood makes you go apeshit, expect a spear through the neck."

I shrug and chomp down on a tentacle. The sudden rush of synthetic battery taste tremor-blasts down my spine and coils spider web patterns in my belly. My eyes water me blind and my face puckers citrus-sour but I don't want the others to know how god-awful this really tastes. "It's not so bad," I squeak.

"Bullshit," someone says.

I'm too busy dry-heaving to know who. There's nothing to vomit except red and green muck. All the walking must have squeezed my body dry. For a minute I wonder how a Christmas elf crawled inside my stomach. Around me unfold mad scenes where Santa's using me as an incubator and injecting me with elf spores and dragging my screaming mind to the North Pole and . . . but then the dry heaves cease and with them, the delirium vanishes.

Faces hover over me. I curl up in fetal position beside the Christmas puke and rub my eyes to see more clearly. Ira, Ancestor, Wayne, Rattlesnake Doctor, Anton, and Sturgeonwolf all stand over me, the bastards. Everyone except for Donkey. In the gap between Ira's legs and Wayne, I spot Donkey. He looks over his shoulder and reaches a hand to his lips. He's guilty as hell. "What's he eating?" I say.

"What is who eating?" Wayne says.

"He's fucked off his tit," Ira says.

Despite my weakened state, I manage to point an accusing finger at Donkey. Everyone turns to face him. He's too dumb to have moved elsewhere after I caught him in the act.

I shut my eyes and wrap my arms around myself. Now that we've stopped walking, the freezing air stings to the bone. Donkey hee-haws desperately.

"You had pancake mix and didn't tell us?" Ira cries.

I open my eyes again. That sorry bastard deserves a real thrashing. I'd get up and whoop him myself if I had the strength. Maybe they'll crucify him. Christ, what a show that would be . . . Donkey bawling and hollering and bleeding his stink all over everyone. He's probably too heavy to hang from a few nails. The nails would tear right through him. They should hang him instead.

Rattlesnake Doctor snickers and walks away from them. He crouches beside me and pulls out a bottle of venom. He takes a swig and offers me the snake bone flask, which I decline. "Suit yourself," he says. "I don't see how so many of you operate without this stuff."

"Like Ira said, we don't have the freaky snake mojo going on."

Once in a while, Rattlesnake Doctor gets this urge to twist our beliefs in ways that incorporate snakes. Why he stays with Yahweh's Dawn instead of becoming a snake-handling (and government-funded) Baptist makes no sense to me. I guess he just wants us to consider things from different angles. He's certainly devoted to our God. His sermons attest to that. Regardless, I want the Flagellation of Donkey, not the Parable of the Prodigal Snake.

I tune Rattlesnake Doctor out as he rambles on about the benefits of drinking venom and how Moses is a thirty-foot rattler who lives in a cave in Afghanistan.

Now feeling remarkably better than I did pre-vomit, I prop myself on an elbow and look around. The red glow of the flowers remains the only source of light. I can't see the other priests, can't believe they've managed to disappear in the short time it's taken for Rattlesnake Doctor's small talk to piss me off so much that I feel a fever coming on.

Something crashes with a clankety-clank beside me. I flip onto my back and scream to alert the others. The laughter of Wayne and Ancestor rings out across the clearing. "What's going on? What do you cocksuckers want?" I say, sobs choking up in my throat.

All the priests appear again. Normal, alive. "It's just some wood," Ancestor says.

"We found a match on Donkey," Wayne says. "It will be wise to get a fire going."

Donkey chortles and says, "We're going to make pancakes. We'll share them with everyone."

Ancestor grunts and walks away, which means the pancake mix contains some animal product, or else we're about to cook the squid-flowers.

Everyone except Ira and Ancestor agrees that mixing the flower blood with pancake mix will mask some of the bitter flavor and result in the greatest quantity of food. Anton explains how at high temperatures certain toxins convert into less toxic chemicals, so it's agreed that cooking the glowing batter over the fire should also be safer than eating it raw.

Ira and Sturgeonwolf, who has no need for nourishment beyond his own sturgeon flesh, start the fire as the rest of us pile squid-flowers into the satchel of pancake mix.

The fire grows to a full blaze as we finish mixing the syrupy blood batter. Looking slightly stupider than usual, Donkey says, "Does anyone have a frying pan?"

"I've got one," Ira says. She tears a razor page from her Jerry and flings it at Donkey, who gapes helpless as the blade spins toward him.

The razor-edged page slams into Donkey's chest plate. He looks down at the blade jutting out of his armor, up at Ira, and then at the batter. "I hope I'm not dead," he says. "I hope I'm not dead."

Ancestor paces over to Donkey and pulls the page from the rusted armor. He rubs his ape hands over the damaged breastplate and flashes a crocodile grin. "Didn't even pierce the armor," he says, and flings the page into the darkness.

"You can't do that," Ira screams. "That was mine."

Ancestor turns and sizes her up, Ira's forehead barely level with his chest. "For that, they should cook you instead of those animals," he says.

Donkey leans over to me and whispers, "What animals? Does he mean the pancakes?"

"You dimwit," I whisper back, "Ancestor's vegan. He doesn't eat animal parts."

"Yeah, but what animals?"

I slap Donkey upside the head and he scampers his fat ass away from me. Wayne steps between Ira and Ancestor. I point my finger and laugh. It's a real fake laugh because I don't feel like laughing and who cares anyway.

Although I think of the squid-flowers more as a plant or fungus, it doesn't surprise me that Ancestor views them as animals. For all his battlefield brutality, he's a total jackass when it comes to food. Once, when he discovered that an apple orchard sprayed their supposedly organic apples with pesticide, he burned down the orchard and locked the owner in a basement full of scorpions. That's one of the reasons you don't cross Ancestor, especially when it comes to food.

We cook the pancakes by laying them out on leaves placed around the fire. Eventually the shitcakes, as Anton calls them, darken to a golden red. The squid-flowers already made me sick once, but I'm hungrier than ever and see little reason to give a damn about health risks at this point. Even Ira and Rattlesnake Doctor break down and eat a few of the flaky discs. I guess that's what starvation does to people.

"So what will we do tomorrow?" Ira says.

Wayne twirls his wooden tail-wand in spirals. "We're going to find Adam and Eve."

"That's if they haven't been eaten by sharks," Ancestor says.

"They've lived among the sharks for so long. They must be fine," Wayne says. He doesn't sound so sure of himself.

Ira looks at both of them. "And if we can't find them?"

"Then we'll kill ourselves," I say.

Wayne flashes me a stunned, forehead-wrinkled stare. What? As if they haven't thought the same thing. "We've got nothing left but each other," I say, "and none of us is a ship that can travel through hyperspace. There's also the question of food and water. Ancestor can protect us against just about anything except God, and hell, maybe we'll find God and he'll lend us a hand for once. Rattlesnake Doctor and Ira are also strong fighters, and Donkey is great with a shotgun. . . ."

I trail off. Something is happening, happening

all around me and I don't know what. My jaw tightens and numbing prickle-points flutter from my toes to my skull, zapping it all to Christmas and back like mosquito lanterns exploding. The others appear dissatisfied. Have I upset them?

A gloved hand descends from the sky and opens my skull with a can opener. The hand pours the contents into a large Tupperware bowl.

"What's a baboon?" Donkey says.

"Fuck a baboon," I say.

"What's wrong with him?" Ira says. She's close to hysterics.

"It's you," I say. "I'm sick of you." I lean back and dig my hands into the blue dirt, waiting for the hand to stir my brain to gray pulp. The remaining squid-flowers melt and pulse around me. The boundary between my flesh and theirs disintegrates. They melt into me.

Wayne says something like, "These flowers could be angels for all we know."

I close my eyes and say, "Is Paradise really paradise?"

Nobody answers.

Suddenly and out of nowhere, the blue sand swallows me and ejects my body into the air. On the way down, my body dissolves into the chirping cricket trees and I fall, I fall and I plunge into a green ocean where mannequins swim instead of fish.

Down there I resolve never to surface again.

CHAPTER THREE
Carcharodon Crush

Ira slugs the fucking hell out of my gut. I've got my arms wrapped around her and my fingers dig into her back. She squirm-thrashes to get away. "What the hell is wrong with you?" she says.

What a way to begin the morning. From last night, I hardly remember anything except for a dream about the Dracula Slugfish dragging me beneath the ground. In the dream, they told me something important. I don't remember what. I forget everything important in dreams.

Years ago, days after joining Yahweh's Dawn, I walked into the monastery and found myself back home, in the bathroom. A manatee shaped as a lobster claw stood in the bathtub, holding a fishing pole. As I entered, it shoved the fishing pole down the drain as if to hide it from me. I looked into the mirror. My reflection didn't look back. Instead I saw a black eel wearing a white glove on its skull. The eel opened its mouth and shrieked like ten thousand blenders grinding bad mood glass. I raised my hands to cover my ears and discovered that seahorses had replaced my ears. I tore away the seahorses and gurgled death like mouthwash. After I died, in the dream, everything the eel said made perfect sense. And then I woke up.

That's the essential disappointment, the shame we feel after we dream. You always wake up. Or maybe what the eel and the Dracula Slugfish have tried to tell me is that no one is wise and nothing is worth knowing. Is that what this is about? Is that even Ira's problem this morning?

Ira makes a display of walking away from me and helps Ancestor rip Dracula Slugfish from his flesh. "Is everything fine?" I call.

"Your dolls are chewing holes in me," Ancestor says, holding up his right arm. Near his wrist, blood leaks from a circular wound the size of a hamburger patty. He crocodile-grins real ugly. "Looks like you can't escape mosquitoes anywhere."

As impressed as I am that the man-beast feels no physical pain, it's too damn obvious that his spiritual weaknesses attracted the Dracula Slugfish to his blood in the first place. I step over to Wayne, who is sleeping near the pile of ash and embers left over from last night's fire. Suddenly my stomach lurches, as if it's dived into a bucket of laxative-soaked barbed wire. I buckle over and puke on the sleeping Wayne.

Sturgeonwolf hurries over. "You feeling alright?" he says. He claps a sturgeon hand across my back.

I collapse, in part because my legs won't support me but also to evade Sturgeonwolf's touch.

Ira crouches beside Ancestor and pukes. He smiles on, pleased that we are all so sick.

My tomato-colored vomit makes Wayne's eyelashes all glossy and drips down his beard . Covered in the junk, he springs alert and pukes on me in retribution. Wizard head vomit comes out slithery and brown, a real decadent slimeball. You could mistake it for crushed earthworms.

I shit in my robe as Anton awakes and pukes on the dozing Doctor. Since Rattlesnake Doctor is so immune to poison and hasn't caught the sickness, he's got to jab a finger down his throat to vomit back at Anton. Ancestor laughs while Sturgeonwolf dashes from priest to priest, asking if we're alright and do we need anything. It's a wonder nobody pukes on him. Then again, who would want him to return the favor?

This entire time, Donkey manages to remain sleeping. Sturgeonwolf shakes him awake and asks how he feels. "Fine," Donkey says, looking bewildered at the condition of the rest of us. Since Donkey's regular diet consists of things like moldy rye bread, it doesn't surprise me that his stomach tolerates the toxic plant juice. The bumbling idiot sits on the blue sand and cleans his three-piece shotgun. For the first time I envy him.

The purge continues for another hour. Then Ancestor forces us to get up and move on anyway. Not far from our camp, smoke coils into the sky. Whoever it is might be gone if we hesitate to move. "If any beasties come," Ancestor says, flexing his bodybuilder muscles, "I'll pound them out of Paradise."

And so we set out on another hike through the forest, puking every step of the way.

Wayne ceases vomiting before the rest of us. He attributes this to self-healing wizard genes, but it probably has more to do with his not having a stomach. At least, I don't see how he could have a stomach, being only a head on stumpy legs. "Before we get to wherever we're going," he says, "did anyone else notice anything peculiar about the squid-flowers? That perhaps squid-flower might not be the proper term for them at all?"

Ira groan-blups. She still has to stop every ten yards or so to puke. She wipes a string of purple saliva from her chin and says, "I don't want to hear another metaphysical conspiracy, you fool."

Wayne must be too caught up in his bullshit to hear her. "Think about it," he says, "half squid and half rose. What might the rose represent? Man, of course. And if the rose is man, then the squid is an angel. That means the squid-flowers are Nephilim, the half-angel, half-human entities mentioned in—"

"There's no mention of the Nephilim being in Paradise Garden," I say.

"Of course not. Why would they be mentioned in Seg Genesis? It makes sense that God left them out."

I stop, not to vomit this time but to process his superhero leap of logic. "You're telling me that beings who are the result of angels mating with humans began to exist before or at the same time as humans?"

Wayne grunts and flicks his tail. He must be pissed now.

"We apologize for being dumb in the ways of sorcery, great Occult Master," Anton says.

Rattlesnake Doctor snicker-hisses. Along with Donkey, he feels no effects from the pancakes, probably because he drinks so much venom every day. Poison counteracting poison? I would ask him about it but Wayne is in one of his Dr. Occult moods where every statement appears to him as a question in need of a lecture-length response on subliminal sea monsters in the Jerry, how vampires invented cyberspace to communicate with the Martian Antichrist, or how the Buddha and his sect of Zen warriors unleashed psychic warfare on the dinosaurs, which is how Wayne explains all mass extinctions anyway. I guess we're fortunate that Wayne acts this way only once or twice every month. We would murder him if he lectured this way all the time.

Sturgeonwolf yelps behind me. I turn around and see that he's tripped over a five-foot sturgeon growth jutting from his hip. None of the others acknowledge the fall in any way. How people treat him, or rather how they don't, you'd think Sturgeonwolf was a ghost. I know less about him than I know about all the other priests, and yet I probably know him better than the others do. Even living and worshipping together doesn't protect some people from their own obscurity, from tripping over themselves just to be reminded they exist.

Maybe fifty yards away, black smoke twists and curls from two wrecked ships. One of the ships is so mangled that at first I think it must be two separate ships, but there's only a single cockpit. A few hours ago, the ship must have glistened red, as if a crew of house painters came by and coated it in layer after layer of blood. Now it's a dark ugly color and flies swarm the fake-looking body parts that inhabit the ship's ambit like human sprinkles on a mechanical cupcake.

Anton flicks out his two foot-long butterfly knives and marches ahead of everyone. He approaches the first mass of mangled electronics and twitters like a bird. "It's an RTC climate alteration ship," he says. "This is bad news. They're specially equipped to defend against sharks. If they've been taken down . . . this is just bad news."

"What does it mean?" I say.

Anton twirls one of his butterfly knives shut. "It means there isn't going to be any way out of Paradise Garden. We're fucked."

"You don't know that," Wayne says.

"Maybe the climate crew survived," Ira says. She walks away and heads toward the second ship, which appears to be in considerably worse condition than the first.

Anton pockets his knives. "Our ship was constructed entirely from parts discarded by the certified factories because of errors, damage, and surplus. I trusted the Gibarian to get us virtually anywhere in hyperspace, and to the closest outlying regions such as Paradise Garden, but I worked under the assumption that government issues were the most error-free machines ever created. As you can see, they're not. All things considered, our best bet is to take what we need and repair the Gibarian."

"What if the crew returns?" Wayne says.

Anton beats a fist against the ship's hull. "They wouldn't be getting anywhere in this thing anyway," he says.

"If you're certain about that, I suppose we can break into groups and salvage what we can," Wayne says. "But we shouldn't need the Gibarian anyway. Not after we find Adam and Eve."

"I'll help Ira explore the other ship," I say, not caring to hear Anton blabber like a know-it-all.

Sturgeonwolf shambles after me, waving a sturgeon hand in the air. I ignore him. He catches up anyway. "We're not getting out of here alive," I say.

He looks at me like he doesn't understand my words. He lowers his fishy werewolf head and coughs.

Ira carries a wooden box out of a hole in the ship's side. "There's someone in there," she says. "I think he's dead."

"What's in the box?" I ask.

"None of your business. See if the guy in there is still alive."

26

"Didn't you—"

She scowls at me and hops down. My breath catches in my lungs.

Sturgeonwolf and I climb through the hole as Ira creeps away with the mysterious box.

As we enter the ship, the sour scent of whiskey burns my nose. Carrying liquor, it must be a supply ship tagging along with the other, as there are none of the egg-shaped incubators like the ones in the Gibarian and all other ships intended for occupation. Having a designated supply ship means their crew must be at least twice the size of ours. Where did they go? Where *could* they go?

I crouch into the ship's silver corridor, the ceiling no more than three or four feet high. Stacked along every wall are wooden crates identical to the one Ira stole. About half the cases have tumbled from the stacks. Busted glass and golden liquid decorate the floor like some Mardi Gras holocaust. I grab an unbroken bottle from the crate nearest me and read the label. Carcharodon Whiskey. "What kind of climate alteration ship needs this much whiskey?" I say.

"I guess it keeps better than water," Sturgeonwolf says.

Donkey crawls into the ship, out of breath from pulling himself through the hole. "They told me to find you and help out," he says, almost apologetic. "Hey, who's that?"

I turn around and trip over a crate. A gray and very wrinkled man sits on broken crates behind me, although I hesitate to say the man *sits* because something ate his legs. "Ira mentioned seeing someone in here. She didn't know if he was alive or dead."

"Looks dead to me," Donkey says.

"Well fucking find out," I say.

He hesitates for a moment, perhaps hoping Sturgeonwolf will do it, then crawls to the back of the ship where the man lies among the broken crates. Donkey pokes the man's shoulder a few times, progressively harder. On the seventh poke, the man's eyes flicker open. Donkey reels back and topples over a crate. "He's alive! Why is he alive?" he says.

I grip a bottle by the neck in case the cripple lunges for us.

The man's eyes dart madly from Donkey to Sturgeonwolf to me. He scrunches up his face and sobs into his hands. "The great white beast in the sky," he mutters, "it took my legs. I didn't do nothing and it took 'em clean off."

His face caves in on itself. The skull sucks his face-flesh in through his mouth cavity. Then his head returns to normal. "Kill me now," he says.

"Donkey, how much ammo do you have left?" I ask, straining to keep my voice steady in the presence of a freak like this guy.

Donkey fumbles through one of his satchels and frowns. "Six shells," he says, "but I can kill him in one shot. I'll shoot him from right here and he'll die the same as if I were holding the gun to his head."

"Save the bullets," I say. "Kill him some other way."

Donkey hee-haws and shuffles toward the legless man. He slides his shotgun from its shoulder holster and rears back with the butt to break the man's nose. "Wait," the man says, "wait."

The gun crushes his face. Bone shards, brain, and buzzing horseflies gush out. The flies swarm into a ghost shape above the corpse. "Wait," say the flies, "wait."

Donkey drops his shotgun and dashes for the exit. He trips and falls before getting there.

"Wait," the flies say.

Sturgeonwolf slaps his prehistoric fins over his

28

eyes. I raise the whiskey bottle and shuffle forward to grab Donkey's gun. Without tearing my sight from the ghost, I toss the gun back to Donkey, who trembles on the deck in a puddle of whiskey and glass.

"What do you want from us?" I say.

The flies buzz spooky spirit sounds. I back away, figuring they want to waste our time. "You should know," they say, pausing to howl more ghost gibberish, "you should know why we came."

"Do you have to speak like that?" I say.

"This ghost thing isn't easy," the flies say. "Let's see how well you communicate with beings who breathe and make love and dream."

I lower the bottle. The ghost is no more of a threat than all the people who waste my time. "Can you tell me what the Right Time Consortium is doing in Paradise Garden? There were no announcements of a climate mission."

"It's the sharks," the ghost says.

"The sharks?"

"They're overtaking Paradise Garden. We're here to alter the climate to kill them off."

"Do Adam and Eve know about this? You could kill off damn near everything in this rotten place. Are you aware of that?"

"Don't look to me for answers. I was only a pilot. At least, I—oh God, I feel it coming. The great white—"

WHAM! Whatever this great white beast is slams into the ship's side. As I hit the deck, my forehead collides against a cracked whiskey bottle and cuts me. The bottle I'm holding slips from my grip as I raise my hands to protect my eyes from all the shattered glass. I close my eyes. SLAM! A crate tumbles near my head and busts wide open, splashing whiskey in my eyes.

29

Minutes pass. When my eyes open, the fly-ghost has vanished.

From outside, Wayne and Ancestor shout. I push myself up from the floor, drenched in liquor from head to toe. Glass shards bite into my palms. I'm a slippery, bloody mess. Wayne crawls through the entrance. He yells, "Is anyone here? Is everyone alright?"

"What the hell was that?" I say, opening a utility closet in search of the ghost.

"We were carrying a tool chest from the other ship when Rattlesnake Doctor spotted a shark circling this one. It head-butted the side and prepared for a second pass when Ancestor tossed a spear. He grazed a fin and the shark flew away. I've never seen anything fly so fast." He flicks his tail at Donkey and says, "Bury that man before we set off again."

Without another word, he marches off the ship. I shake my head and help Donkey carry the mutilated torso outside. We set the body down and I leave Donkey to bury it. Ancestor, Rattlesnake Doctor, and Anton stand on lookout for sharks. Sturgeonwolf must still be on the ship or he's gone off by himself. I consider talking to Wayne about what the pilot told me, but then Sturgeonwolf howls from behind the supply ship.

Sturgeonwolf leans over Ira's body, which slumps against the trunk of a massive tree. She babbles and demon-shrieks, slurring about how at the next Last Supper, Jesus will eat pancakes and drink whiskey. The way she handles liquor, I should have known she would haul the crate off to get drunk somewhere. Still, I can't feel that guilty. When Ira has an end in mind, she doesn't give a shit how she achieves it, and she only accepts one way: her own.

Wayne turns to me and says, "Do you have any holy water? We need to perform an exorcism."

I shrug. "She's drunk. An exorcism would be stupid. It might kill her."

Inch-deep gashes line her arms. Thinned by the liquor, her blood gushes out in spurts. Not the worst she's ever cut herself, but pretty bad all the same. "The word made flesh," she moans, "I am the word made flesh."

"We've got to leave her behind," Ancestor says. "The sharks will detect her blood from miles away. They will follow us all the way back to the Gibarian."

Donkey approaches, wiping dirt from his hands. He says, "Does anyone have a key? I've lost mine."

I reach into the pocket of my bathrobe and pull out a small golden key. "Even here you still have to bury bodies with a key?" I say.

"Thanks," Donkey says, snatching the key. He shuffles away, his hunchback towering a foot over his head.

Far away in the cloudless green sky and just above the tree line, a slender shark flies toward us. No one speaks as it approaches. I stare down at Ira and realize that it is far too late for any of us to hide.

Ancestor calls for everyone to gather. Ira cries for the blood of Christ. She's so pitiful right now, so close to being a saint of whiskey and self-mutilation. With the sun low-low in the sky, I transform into toad form and wait for the worst.

CHAPTER FOUR
Sharkquake

The great white shark must be ten feet long.

It circles the wreckage several times before swooping down for an attack. Ancestor stands poised for battle, a bamboo spear in his raised right hand, ready to throw at near-lightspeed velocity. He twirls his battleaxe in the other hand.

The shark lunges, its open jaws revealing row upon row of razor-sharp teeth. We cower behind Ancestor, embracing one another in stomach-flipping terror. Hunting sharks in this manner is not what we signed up for, not at all.

Ancestor tosses the spear straight into the shark's mouth. The beast charges anyway, undamaged and thrashing its tail in epileptic windmills. Ancestor spins away from the massive tail. He swings his axe full circle and severs the shark's head.

No one moves.

Eyes dilated from dreadfearanxiety, we scan the sky for more sharks. Wayne offers to lead us in group prayer. Since landing in Paradise Garden, I've prayed only once. As we say a few Our Father's aloud, I wonder if the others have also neglected prayer.

Anton pulls a bottle of whiskey from Ira's crate. He unscrews the lid, tosses it over his shoulder, and drinks a healthy swig. Donkey takes a few swigs of his own and then the bottle ends up in my hands. I tip the bottle toward Wayne. He shakes his head and his face reddens but he does nothing to stop us. I tilt the bottom of the bottle to the sky, careful to swig more than Anton and Donkey. From me, the bottle goes to Rattlesnake Doctor and then Wayne caves in and has a drink himself. "We've still got to perform the exorcism," he says.

"It won't do anything," Anton says, "and now that we know the sharks are weaklings, let's celebrate. Ancestor can fight them off if more arrive."

Ancestor crouches beside the headless shark. He cradles the massive head like it's a wounded comrade. I gulp a few more mouthfuls of whiskey and stagger up to him. "Everything fine?" I say. The whiskey filters through my blood, sweeping the anxiety from my mind.

He stands and gives me this look like I just walked in on him shitting. "I don't see the reason behind this shark dying," he says.

"Because otherwise it would have killed *us*," I say.

He strokes the shark's head and says, "And what makes us more important? What if it was God's will for this shark to kill us?"

"Well buddy," I throw up my arms in a *darn, wish I could help you* manner, "we came to Paradise Garden to hunt sharks. If you've got beef with asserting your dominion over the animal kingdom, you should have said so. We'd have been happy to let you stay at the monastery and, I don't know, knit curtains." To say you've got beef with someone is a lousy term that no one older than thirteen should ever use, but I know the meat reference will irritate Ancestor.

I shift from foot to foot and reposition my top hat. It's a wonder Ancestor doesn't smash my face in. He must really be devastated about killing this shark. He's never really revealed this side of himself to me, never questioned his actions in battle, never really questioned much at all. I mean, of course I respect him as much as I respect everyone, especially my fellow priests, but Ancestor always gave me the impression of being nothing more than a noble savage, devoid of conscience despite his dietary choices. I say, "If it was God's will, we would be dead."

He shakes his head. "What God wants isn't always what happens."

"How can you know that?" I say.

"Unless there is no free will, then God's will cannot be absolute, and the absence of free will means that all of us are like your mannequins. You can only take action if you are free, otherwise you just react."

"But isn't our will also God's will?"

"You might live your life according to the divine plan, but that is a choice you make. The moment you or anyone else deviates from that, God's will becomes less than absolute. What I feel right now is that I should not have killed this shark. Something tells me we were supposed to die right here."

I shrug. I'm about to tell Ancestor why his ideas are bullshit when the ground tremors harder than any earthquake I've ever felt. I'm swept off my feet.

The rumbling continues for several minutes. I scramble to my knees and try to decipher whatever Wayne and the other priests are yelling. Rattlesnake Doctor points a finger. I scramble away as a shark head emerges from the blue sand and eats Anton. The shark's head must be larger than the entire shark that Ancestor murdered. The sand splashes over us, stinging my eyes. Where the shark arises, the sand gives

34

way and Anton vanishes into a shark tooth abyss. Three feathers from Anton flutter to the ground. As quickly as the sharkquake deafened the land, the shark's lunatic jaws vacuum up all the noise in Paradise Garden. The silence leaves me homesick and lonely. My heart beats, beats beats, beats, beats beats, beats so bad it hurts.

The shark sinks back into the ground so that just its nose pokes out, then it bursts out of the hole and into the sky. Sand rains down on us like particle matter flung across the cosmos by God on the first day of the universe.

The shark flies thousands of feet in the air. It must be fifty feet long. I recall once reading about megalodon, the giant prehistoric shark. Considering the size of this shark, that's what it must be, which means the first shark was only a baby. I tear my eyes from the downward-spiraling shark in time to see Wayne and Donkey hustle for cover in the forest. Rattlesnake Doctor scoops Ira into his arms and shouts for the rest of us to follow quick. I dash after him and am soon on his heels.

We hide behind trees, waiting for Ancestor. Sturgeonwolf waddles from behind his tree and onto the battlefield. Hardly a proficient fighter, what he's doing is insane.

The shark must sense this weakness. Like a multi-bladed machete, it cleaves every sturgeon growth from Sturgeonwolf's body in seconds. A soupy fur ball, his werewolf-fishy flesh glistens in the light of the black daylight sun. The corpse of Sturgeonwolf falls to the sand. He's uglier and deader than ever. I almost pity the poor scumsucker.

The megalodon writhes in the air and charges. Ancestor tosses a bamboo spear. Before this superior creature, his spears are frail and inadequate. It bounces off the shark's nose. He might as well have flicked a toothpick at it.

Ancestor drops his spear bundle and swings into battle stance, axe raised and ready. Just by twitching its tail, the megalodon reduces ten trees to splinters.

The shark charges again. Ancestor swings with everything he's got. It's not enough. The shark eats him, weapons and all, in one bite. On the battlefield, nothing remains of the great warrior except his legs—his feet up to his kneecaps—as we take flight through the forest.

Wayne leads the way through the forest as the shark, less than one hundred yards behind us, decimates every tree in its path. Donkey hee-haws and sniffles. He trips over fallen branches and kills what little hope I possess that we might survive to live another day, let alone the span of half an hour. Rattlesnake Doctor falls behind too. He can't carry Ira for much longer. I'm out of breath and yell for Wayne to slow down. The little fucker is too fast for us. Donkey stumbles ahead until I lose sight of him. We have to find some more efficient way to haul Ira.

The ground feels like it might collapse any moment. A giant pine topples over and blocks our path. Over the roar of the world, Rattlesnake Doctor says, "I'll boost you up."

He forms a web with his hands. I step into it with my left foot and claw at the tree. "Higher," I yell, as more trees uproot all around us. "I can't get a grip!"

Rattlesnake Doctor hisses as he looks over his shoulder. His extrasensory reptile instincts must indicate that the shark is closing in. He musters strength and boosts my left leg higher and higher until I manage to secure a hold in a hollow some animal must have used for a nest. I pull myself onto the fallen trunk and stare down at him. Rattlesnake Doctor bends over and scoops Ira into his arms. He lifts her above his head. His slim arms shake from the strain. "Take her," he says, neck veins bulging green. "You'll be fine."

I open my mouth to tell him not to be a tricky bastard. It's too late. A white tail as tall as the trees reduces everything behind Rattlesnake Doctor into dust and tree pulp. I wrap my arms around Ira's waist and pull her onto the trunk. She lies unconscious beside me. I turn back to Rattlesnake Doctor. I yell, "Take my hand, goddamn you."

He flicks his tongue and stumbles backwards, tears blurring his snake eyes. The shark's tail fans back and forth in rhythmic rotations. The shark turns as if to peek over its shoulder, its obsidian eyes larger than horses. Dust devils stir up in the wake of that tail. Rattlesnake Doctor takes a long swig from his flask of venom and tosses it at the shark. I see what he's doing now. All that poison coursing through his veins, I bet he figures he can save the rest of us by playing the sacrificial lamb. A pang of guilt rises in me for not treating him differently, but with it comes relief.

He slips his snake tamer flute from its ivory case and plays a tune. He marches funeral style toward the shark's endless rows of razorblade tombstones. At the very end of his march, when he's about to step into the shark's mouth, he turns. He's changed his mind. It isn't worth it. I see what he sees. I see that courage gets you nowhere. It's too late. He vanishes into the mouth. Anyway, no one is brave.

An infernal grumbling rises from the shark's stomach. The poison must be effective and fast-acting. I shake myself out of the death vision and hoist Ira over my shoulder. I jump from the tree and hope not to drop her.

Wayne and Donkey stand on the other side of the tree. Donkey waves his arms like a proud idiot. Wayne holds an extra long shoelace in his mouth. Donkey takes it from him and ties Ira to my back as if I'm a slippery, amphibious horse. The shoelace securely knotted, we hurry on, squeezing through vegetation that only gets more suffocating as we forge a new path.

The black sun falls and casts us into another night, but I don't transform back into human form. I've sensed the sickness growing inside me since the morning, but only become conscious of it now. Something in me must have known. Otherwise I would have tried to turn the shark into a mannequin. If I didn't try, it's not because I was afraid. It's because something in me knew. It had to be.

This has only happened once before, when I contracted intestinal parasites four years ago. I picked up a real bad case of them. The worms dissolved my insides and transformed me into a sleepless, diarrheic wreck until Wayne identified the problem with the assistance of one of his medieval alchemy volumes. A wormwood and garlic treatment worked wonders, but I don't suppose either are available to me in Paradise Garden. If we ever find Adam and Eve, it will be a priority of mine to ask. Without any cure on hand, I wonder what will become of me. If I'm trapped in this body for too long, will amphibious thoughts invade and dissolve my essential humanness? I envision myself abandoning the others and starving to death in a cold swamp in the darkest part of the forest. If God were to send a princess my way, maybe she'd kiss me and my seed could populate a new earth. I'm fit for the role of Adam. I've got solid genes, really the best variety.

The forest ends.

We tumble down a rocky cliff. Crumbly rocks scratch and bruise me all the way down. After the long fall, we land dog pile at the edge of a flat clearing, mere feet from taking a potentially fatal drop. The darkness prevents me from calculating how far we fell, but hiking or scaling back up the cliff is probably impossible.

I rub my head. Blood dampens my hairline, but the cut from the whiskey bottle doesn't feel serious. Head wounds just bleed a lot.

"Where did you assholes put my Jerry?" Ira screams, conscious again but apparently unaware that we just fell off a cliff.

Wayne appears sorrier and more decrepit than ever. "You passed out," he huffs, "and then we were attacked."

"Look at that," Donkey says. He points to a cave entrance in the cliff wall and when we say nothing, he hurries over to it. He walks inside. We listen as Donkey bellows out three hellos from within the cave. "It's empty," he calls.

Wayne and I get up and scramble toward it. Ira, seeing how desperate we are for shelter, limps after us. We crawl to the back of the cave and huddle in a tight circle. Ira says, "What's going on?"

"I've got stomach parasites," I say.

"Again? Now?" Wayne says.

"The squid-flowers," I say, "it must have been the squid-flowers. All of you should be fine. It's me that's got to suffer and be a shitty toad until we find Adam and Eve or get the hell out of this place."

"Will someone tell me what the fuck is going on?" Ira says.

As Wayne explains everything, my thoughts drift and I think about God. My thoughts about God are always vague, more of a blurry tingling on the back of my neck.

When Wayne finishes, Ira says, "At least we ditched the snake freak."

"He saved our lives," I say.

"It served him right to sacrifice himself for a bunch of incompetents," Ira says. "I can't believe you've fucked everything up so bad. What about all your spells, Wayne? Why couldn't you have pulled some magic card out of your ass? And your mannequin power, what about that, Ernest? God, how I wish I could turn back time to before I met any of you."

I point a finger at her. "Ira, lay off him. You're an icy bitch and everyone here is doing the best they can to tolerate it. Rattlesnake Doctor saved your ass. If that doesn't shut you up, I don't know what to say."

"So glad I need a lecture from Mr. Right, is that it? You've got no say in what I think. I've seen you stare out at us so smug and satisfied, thinking you're so magnificent. Let me tell you, you're not, and you smell like swamp ass when you're a toad. It's none of your business if I think Wayne's an idiot. You're all idiots."

Wayne is sensitive about his powers. Ira knows this, but she's drunk. Wayne lowers his head to the cave floor and closes his eyes. He weeps to himself. Wayne's spells might be worthless, but they're really no worse than the epic fantasy series he used to write. Every time a new book came out, he destroyed a copy and used the pages to construct a paper mache unicorn. He thought, and still thinks, that unicorns are the stupidest fantasy creatures, which they are, but for him these paper mache creatures justified the writing of another book. They made his failures alright. I read Battlesnakes, the first book in the series, and found Wayne's capacity for tasteless fantasy clichés nauseatingly inexhaustible. It's amazing a band of outraged readers didn't seriously fuck him up.

He quits his crying and speaks up, angry now. "You must have faith in God," he says, "or else damn you, damn you all!"

Donkey pats Wayne's head like he would an old dog. "We'll be fine," he says. "Before my grandma and grandpa shot themselves, they made me promise to open a holy pancake house. I never did it and sometimes I am sad because their ghosts can't rest for what I've done. When we get back to where we belong, we can all do it together. We can even call the pancake house Yahweh's Dawn, if you like. I believe it can happen, and I bet God does too."

I want to tell Donkey that we won't be returning, that at this point our survival rate hangs a notch below zero. I want to crush his hope, but it makes me afraid to consider what might happen if I fracture Donkey's naïve trust in happy endings. We might all shrivel up and die, hopeless and forlorn. Besides, unless he's a more profound idiot than I take him to be, his bubble of hope will burst soon enough.

A dark form rushes by the cave entrance, blocking all the light that reaches us, huddled as we are at the back of the cave. It passes again and again, each time shutting us in total black for intervals of ten, thirty, sixty seconds. Ira whispers a prayer. Wayne and Donkey join in. I clasp my hands but fail to utter any words.

CHAPTER FIVE
Out of the Cave

We close our eyes and try discovering comfortable positions on the pebbly floor. The dark thing scuff-shuffles out there in the night and keeps us too paranoid to accomplish much shut-eye. Considering the stomach parasites, I doubt I could sleep anywhere without the wormwood and garlic concoction or a sedative like alcohol. If we fail to find Adam and Eve tomorrow, I'll have to search elsewhere for a cure. After three or four days of sleeplessness, I'll be viewing the world through that anxious-bright-and-melting claustrophobic vision that I acquire during bouts with insomnia. There couldn't be any worse way to face Paradise Garden.

My eyes can't adjust to the cave darkness. I've never felt so eager for the sun to rise. The animal noises echo throughout the cave now. There must be a lot of them. Whatever they are, they're creeping into the cave, inching their way toward us in the darkness. The only creatures I know to prance around on cliffs and make strange farm noises are mountain goats. "Do mountain goats live in Paradise?" I say.

"You moron," Wayne says, "goats don't oink."

Ira stifles an annoyed laugh. "You're both idiots," she says. "Does Donkey have any matches?

"All gone," Donkey says.

Ira sighs. "Then use an illumination spell so we can

see what's going on out there."

"But my magic isn't—"

"Just do it!" Ira says.

The oink-snuffling things must hear her yell. Their scuffles and snuffles are suddenly deafening inside the cave.

"Let me think for a minute," Wayne says.

"We don't have a minute," I say.

Wayne mutters to himself about catfish deserts and Death sleeping with aliens in ancient pyramids. His manic babbling becomes too rapid to decipher and then FLICK. A white lighter materializes. It levitates between us. It doesn't really illuminate the cave, just gives depth and shadow to the pack of black-haired hogs shuffling toward us. The creatures have no back legs. Their hind skeletal system is nothing more than two wheels of bone. It's like the corpses of crippled humans dug themselves out of their graves and discovered they couldn't walk, then decided to kill pigs, hollow them out, and weld themselves to wheelchairs. "Flesh and bone wheelchair hogs," I say, awed by this monstrosity. I imagine these wheelchair hogs pulling themselves along night after night, seeking everlasting filth and discovering only themselves.

"Does anyone have a plan?" Ira says.

All blubbery, Donkey genuflects. He must have dropped his shotgun somewhere, which means we've got no way to defend ourselves against the shambling horde of wheelchair hogs.

"Ever see a zombie film?" Wayne asks.

We all look at him like he's really lost it. Ira raises her right hand to slap him but Wayne steps out of her reach. "In the early movies," he says, "the zombies are so slow and clumsy that the actors can evade them without getting bitten."

"We're not actors," I say.

"Or actresses," Ira says.

Wayne points. "Look how slow these monsters move. We've still got twenty feet between us. If we move now, and I mean right now, we just might come out alive on the other side. Stay low to the ground and dodge between them. It doesn't appear they can bend down very far."

Ira shrugs. "Let's go then, if you want to kill us all." She pushes Wayne and follows directly behind, using him as a shield.

Donkey follows, then myself. The wheelchair hogs smell worse than an outhouse heaping with spoiled calamari. The light produced from his illumination spell doesn't follow us. I bump into the wheelchair hogs as I squeeze between them, which confirms the notion that my power no longer works.

The wheelchair hogs are gooier than they look.

Despite going last, I emerge from the cave at almost the exact moment as Wayne and Ira. We hurry away from the entrance and then halt. Donkey is gone. He must be too much of a lard ass to push through the swarm of hogs.

"We can't wait for him," Ira says.

"No, too many have been lost as it is. We can't afford another casualty," Wayne says.

"And if we all die?" Ira says, hands poised on her hips.

Before Wayne responds, Donkey hee-haws and barges out of the cave. Two wheelchair hogs shuffle after him, but we don't wait for them to catch up as we descend the cliff. The darkness prevents us from moving quicker than inch by inch over the rocky mountainside and I'm amused by the thought that whatever we meet at the bottom might be far worse than the wheelchair hogs. Then again, we might also be closer to Adam and Eve, although I now doubt that they would ever choose to live in such a barren shithole.

Donkey catches up with us. The wheelchair hogs,

awkward as they are, remain in hot pursuit. They're obviously familiar with the terrain.

The cliff levels off to a more even grade and we gain momentum. If we're to lose the hogs, this is where it will happen. Donkeys trips over himself and knocks Wayne down. I crane my head to see if the wheelchair hogs are gaining on us. They stand at the edge of the cliff, oink-snuffling and hesitant to pursue us beyond that point, as if an invisible barrier forbids them from descending the mountain.

"The sky is different now," Wayne says.

The sky above the mountain remains black, but the sky on this side drips algae colors. The air is even colder. We decide to catch our breath before journeying on. I ask Wayne how he thought of the zombie-style escape. He wheeze-laughs and whacks a pile of pebbles with his tail. "It's the monsters, I guess. What it means to be a monster."

I shrug. Heroes, monsters . . . all that fantasy crap never caught my fancy. As a child, I found the natural world far more enrapturing . . . snakes, lizards, spiders, that sort of thing. How I came to religion at all is a tricky, fractured story, but I suppose terrible things happen to everyone. Like Wayne and the rest of Yahweh's Dawn, I've experienced more than my load of evil shit. If I had to decide, I'd say that's what brought us all together in the first place. It's the evil shit that drowns so many of us.

"What the hell are those?" Ira says.

Lobster-shaped cacti tower all around us, but Ira pays no mind to them. She points out a pack of gargoyles, the kind you see perched atop cathedrals, if gargoyles were born out of techno scrap heaps. They gallop horse-like and communicate in beeps and tin foil crumples. One gargoyle resembles a complex computer attached to vacuum cleaner legs. It clutches Ira's Jerry and Donkey's shotgun in its jaws, which are actually two ancient telephones soldered together. Another mechanical creature licks the spines off of a lobster cactus with its pink, human-sized tongue. It is by far the most organic machine among them.

Ira, apparently unthreatened by these creatures, charges the one holding her Jerry. As she approaches, it backpedals and catches its legs on a boulder. She snatches her Jerry and Donkey's shotgun from the old telephone jaws. "Fucking scavengers," she says, punishing the mechanical creatures with her signature pissed-off stare.

She tosses the shotgun to Donkey. Stammering, he opens the barrel and examines the gun's other components and then raises his eyes to the creatures. They appear afraid to get close to us again. "It's fine," Donkey says, as if waiting for someone to step out and says it's all a cruel joke. "Everything is fine."

The creatures howl at the sky and shuffle away, drooping low to the ground. The dawn will be on us soon. "So what now?" I say.

"I suppose we should follow them," Wayne says.

Ira begins to protest but then shuts her trap. She must realize that our only other option is to turn back and retread the nightmares we've already faced.

"Then let's move," she says.

Technology has always been a sensitive topic for me. The creation of machines and the subsequent exploitation of those machines seems wrong. Ancestor and I used to talk about this. He felt that in the near future there would be machine rights activists as well as animal rights activists like himself. For crazy talks like that, I almost miss him now. I'm also concerned that if machines rise to power, God will abandon us and love the machines instead. He might take our souls and give them to the machines.

I shrug and swallow sand-mushy spit. We walk for hours, days . . . who the fuck knows. My legs drag behind me. It's impossible to keep up with Paradise Garden's short nights and shorter days, or maybe the nights just feel longer. I'm still trapped in toad form and count on dehydrating into toad jerky soon. The algae sky quivers, a constant promise of rain that haunts us and never produces.

The sky lightens entirely and its gooiness crusts over.

Wayne swats his tail in the dirt. "This isn't right," he says. "I've thought all these hours and I can't get my mind around it. Paradise Garden is not that big. Adam and Eve should have sensed trouble and rescued us by now. Anyway, they never spoke about machines in Paradise Garden. Those robot creatures might be harmless, but it's unusual for them to be here at all."

"All we really know about Paradise Garden is what Adam and Even have told us," I say. "They could have lied."

Wayne ignores me and mutters to himself. "It just doesn't make sense . . . it makes no sense at all. . . ."

"Maybe God's mechanical and we're fucked," Ira says.

"Blasphemy," Wayne says.

Ira twists his left ear and tells him to shut up. "I've believed in God longer than any of you," she says. She walks away from us, wiping tears from her face.

Wayne and I stare after Ira and then look at each other. I don't think Ira sees what she's walking toward, what the mechanical creatures are gathering around.

I tell myself this is an illusion of Paradise.

CHAPTER SIX
The Tree of Knowledge

The Tree of Knowledge calls his scrap-electrical hyenas Junk Children. For nourishment, his mechanical scavengers rely not only on whatever dead, diseased, and defenseless beings they encounter, but also the ever-replenishing fungal limbs of the Tree of Knowledge. Towering thirty feet tall, the Tree of Knowledge is a crossbreed between a cricket tree and the grays, those big-headed aliens common in abduction reports. That's how Wayne describes the tree. He must be retarded. No one could mistake this tangled, vinegar-smelling blob for a tree, although it is rather extraterrestrial.

Since we're all near the point of collapse and risk getting picked off by the Junk Children if we sleep on the rocky plain, the Tree of Knowledge offers provisions for a night. The shelter, it turns out, is the tree itself.

Ira cuts a door in the gray, semi-translucent trunk with her Jerry. It's all fishy and I've got to clamp my mouth shut to prevent vomit from shoveling out. As we crawl into the tree, new flesh immediately seals the doorway behind us. The stuffy air tastes saltier and the fishiness disappears. Gravity vanishes and we float up, up, up into the skull of the Tree of Knowledge.

Being inside the tree's skull reminds me of a black and white movie, or how it might feel to live inside a black and white movie. Crumpled tin foil sounds irritate my ears.

White spots and other blemishes pop up like a meteor shower of cigarette burns. I open my mouth to ask the others if they feel the same but my tongue feels caught in hardened sap. It won't shape the words.

The crackly-synthetic voice of the Tree of Knowledge speaks. "In my skull, you can only speak through your mind. First, I must plug all of you into the root system. In the meantime you can feast."

I open my eyes. I didn't even know I had closed them. On a blanket in the center of the plastic-walled room sits a basket of fruit, a jug of wine, and a six foot bread loaf coiled up like a snake ready to strike. I approach the blanket and features of the bread become clear: a serpent's head, scales, and even a flickering bread tongue. The snake nods at me as if eager to be eaten. Stomach grumbling, I rip a chunk from its tail. Some sort of green broth oozes from the tail wound. I dip the bread in the broth and shove the soggy glob in my mouth. The others stare on as I swallow the snake food. I nod and give them the thumbs up. The bread and soup, which I think is split pea, taste delicious. I break off another chunk of snake bread and the others hurry to do the same. We dig our fingers into the serpent's belly. Wayne, digging his toes into the bread, suddenly stops us. He nods his head upward until we understand what he means. He wants us to give thanks.

Maybe the others pray, but I don't have the will for it. Anyway, this gift isn't from God. This is from the Tree of Knowledge. My belly doesn't give a shit whether God has anything to do with it, and after all the terrible things that have gone down in Paradise Garden, I'm starting to think that we must register as nothing more than tiny viruses on God's radar.

After five minutes of continuous feasting, we look

up at each other. We nod and rub our bellies, contented and pleasantly disgusted with ourselves, splotched with bread crumbs and pea soup. Next we move on to the fruit and wine. I've never been much of a wine drinker outside of church, but this wine soothes my throat more than any liquid I have ever drank.

We pass the jug around until every drop has been shaken from the bottom. As I settle into drunkenness, the Tree of Knowledge fills my head again. "We may communicate now," he says. "I suggest lying down. My Junk Children report intense nausea when they remain standing during mind dialogues."

"Mind dialogues?" Ira says, or perhaps *thinks* is more accurate.

Apparently feeling the body sickness the tree warned us about, Ira's face contorts and she curls up on the blanket.

Wayne's voice fills my head. "How does this mind dialogue work?"

"Lie down, all of you," says the Tree of Knowledge. "I will tell of many things."

The tree grunts approval as we lie on our backs. It asks us to close our eyes.

Mind Dialogue with the Tree of Knowledge

Tree of Knowledge: Much better.

Ira: What is this?

Tree of Knowledge: A special world I created for my Junk Children, where I can enjoy them.

Me: And the Junk Children are . . . ?

Tree of Knowledge: One of the more primitive machines in Paradise Garden. I love them because they are my creations.

Me: Machines?

Wayne: *Your* creations?

Tree of Knowledge: Did you think God was the only creator? Technology is everyone's friend in Paradise Garden.

Wayne: Adam and Eve invited us. We had an accident. If you'd point us in their direction, or if you could somehow contact them . . .

Tree of Knowledge: Have you met the Tree of Life?

Ira: Look, if you want to play head games then we're leaving. We don't have time for bullshit.

Tree of Knowledge: It is rumored that the Tree of Life is more of a jokester than myself. A matter of perspective, I suppose.

Wayne: If you won't help us find Adam and Eve, can you tell us about God? Is He here in Paradise Garden?

Tree of Knowledge: Nothing here can tell you about God.

Me: Then tell us about the Tree of Life.

Tree of Knowledge: Eager for life, are we? Who is this other mind in my skull?

Wayne: Donkey?

Me: He's shy when he craps himself.

Donkey: (whimpering) Sorry.

Tree of Knowledge: How my Junk Children savor the shit of silent ones. Paradise Garden is not what you think. God is not what you think. In all my days I have seen God only once, and that was enough for me to construct my children. Junk piles, maybe. Alarms, absolutely. I can only hope they alert me soon enough whenever God comes this way.

Me: Why are you the Tree of Knowledge?

Tree of Knowledge: Because I know nothing else.

Wayne: Maybe if you pointed us to the Tree of Life, or at least to the path we should follow, that would be fine. I'm sure we can find Adam and Eve from there.

Tree of Knowledge: But why should you leave so soon? We have games, so many games to play. So many games to derange your perceptions. Would anyone care to sample the sweets growing in my skull? I have savage membrane lollipops, gumdrop leviathans, everything you ever wanted. When you have tasted them, then maybe you will find the path to God or (snickers) Adam and Eve.

Me: How can we be certain that anything you say is true?

Tree of Knowledge: By realizing that nothing is certain or true in Paradise Garden. Have you survived all this time without realizing that?

Ira: Thanks for the food and shelter, but cut the bullshit. We had enough of it where we came from.

Tree of Knowledge: Where you came from . . . I know that place well.

Wayne: Whatever it takes, we'll be returning after—

Tree of Knowledge: Unless I am mistaken, nobody escapes Paradise Garden.

Wayne: We were invited here, and I'm certain that Adam and Eve would have been well aware of that before inviting us.

Tree of Knowledge: Did you come here to hunt sharks?

Wayne: We came here because this is what we believe in.

Tree of Knowledge: If finding some carcass to crawl inside is what you desire, I suggest tracking down the Tree of Life. You can rest beneath her branches forever.

Me: You still haven't told us about the Tree of Life, or even where to look.

Ira: This is what we get for talking to trees. Are you guys finished?

Me: Something is wrong.

Tree of Knowledge: Something is always wrong when you plan for *your* Paradise Garden and find yourself in the Paradise Garden of another . . . in the true Paradise.

Me: Hold up, you said nothing is true.

Tree of Knowledge: Then what does that say about Paradise Garden?

Me: If nothing is true, and this is the true Paradise Garden, then Paradise Garden is nothing?

Wayne: Then Paradise is everything.

Me: Nothing and Everything?

Ira: Fucking trees.

Wayne: Can you at least give us some history about the Tree of Life? We need something, anything.

Tree of Knowledge: You've traveled far for a history lesson. (Pause) I recall everything, except for the sharks. Their origin is unknown to me. For a period, a disastrous amnesia fogged my mind. This amnesia gripped all of Paradise Garden in its hands and never let go. It was during this period that I saw God. Afterward, the sharks emerged from the outerground. Those hands that choked Paradise loosened their stranglehold, but they never let go altogether. First the sharks came for the Tree of Life. For forty days and forty nights they tormented the tree. Every morning, just after dawn, I nurtured the tree with bread and wine. During those days, the tree blossomed leaves of fluorescent glass and grew circuitwire fruit. I imagined my bread and wine to be the cause, but after the fortieth day and night, the sharks roamed elsewhere. The Tree of Life lost its leaves. Its fruit molded until no animals would touch it. I fed it every morning, just before dawn. Day and night I slaved over the design of my junk children. The morning of their creation, I lost hope for the Tree of Life. I lost hope for Paradise Garden. There was nothing left to do but preserve my new creations. They are the sad reminders of the old garden. Memories rust in my brain. If there is something you can save in Paradise, it is the Tree of Life. Not God, not Paradise itself, and certainly not (snickers again) Adam and Eve. The old ways are lost, but who knows? Maybe the tree has one last message to impart to you.

Wayne: What about the sharks? What if we defeat them?

Tree of Knowledge: You cannot defeat them.

Wayne: We can try.

Tree of Knowledge: No use.

Wayne: Neither is letting our dreams die. We'll visit the Tree of Life.

Tree of Knowledge: Your faith and courage are admirable, but the sharks transcended such measures long ago, likely before they overtook Paradise.

Wayne: Don't give up on us.

Tree of Knowledge: I have given up on myself.

Me: Then why go on?

Tree of Knowledge: Because maybe someday I will discover the reason Paradise Garden changed. I want you to dream now. If you dream, I will show you the road to the Tree of Life. If you disobey and crawl out of my skull before morning, the Junk Children will have you as their playthings.

End of Mind Dialogue

I want to discuss the mind dialogue with Wayne and the others, but we lose speech capacity as soon as we're unplugged and it's too dark to communicate through gestures. Maybe I drank too much wine. The room spins like a bat hooked through the wing and getting reeled in by a fishing pole. The last thing I see before dozing off are Junk Children hanging from the walls and grinning at me.

CHAPTER SEVEN
The Mutant Nothing

The farther we venture from the Tree of Knowledge, the more I notice the same tingling sensation that marks my transformation from toad to human. I pass it off as lingering tremors from my nightmares (unless they really happened) of Junk Children. They're creeping behind us now, laughing like the ghosts of sewing machines. I force my attention to the Tree of Life. If we fail to find real help there, I doubt we'll hold out much longer.

"What the hell did that tree do to your hands?" Ira shouts.

Since Wayne doesn't have hands, she can only be speaking to Donkey or me, and Donkey's hands look as fat and ugly as ever.

My hands are part human again but still green, webbed, and tangled like tree limbs. They're also twice as large as normal. I fall to my knees on the ashen path and raise my hands to the algae sky. I'm a mutant nothing. "God," I croak, "why did you do this to my hands?" My voice sounds split, as if two people are speaking at once, one who is a total stranger to me. My brain fogs over.

"Get up, the sun is falling," Wayne says. "According to the map, the Tree of Life should be over the next hill and Junk Children will—"

"We know," Ira snaps.

It always gets my brain buzzing whenever Ira defends me in any way, for any reason. Not that she won't turn around and bitch at me for something else, but at least it lets me know she doesn't always view me as some idiot who would be better off locked in a cage.

Donkey hee-haws and uses his shotgun to nudge away the Junk Child that has been breathing down his neck for the better part of an hour. This one, built of bicycle parts, is even more passive than the other Junk Children. It scoots away to slobber machine grease on a cactus lobster.

"Hurry up, we haven't got the time," Wayne says.

My feet grow more and more oversized as Ira drags me along by my hands. "Get moving or I'll break your legs," she says.

Wayne stops. He asks if I can walk. I stagger a few wobbly steps. My body slumps beneath the weight of my hands. Can't this jerk see I'm entirely incapable of moving any great distance? "If I must," I say.

"Good enough," Wayne says, folding up the map and trudging onward.

Ira yanks me forward. Donkey shuffles behind us, waving his shotgun at the Junk Children. I say nothing, too ashamed to speak in my broken half-toad, half-human voice. I want to ask Wayne if this is how possessed people talk but then we arrive at the last hill.

What we encounter on the other side of the hill is not a tree. I don't see a single tree, shrub, flower, or stick, only more sand and a silver fortress that looks similar to a military base. Considering what little we know about Paradise Garden, I wonder if this construction is the Tree of Life, but someone has splattered the words THIS IS A FORTRESS in black paint on the side of the enormous building.

We stand about fifty yards away. "Maybe Adam and Eve live here," Wayne says, sounding anything but hopeful.

Three skeleton-looking robots burst through a door in the fortress.

Before we can blink, they're demanding that we drop all weapons. I look to Wayne and Ira to see if they want to run for it before the robots can seize us. They don't. "So we've been scammed," I say.

"I could have told you that tree was no good," Ira says.

"Has anyone ever met a robot?" Wayne asks.

Donkey snuffles. He says, "My grandparents once told me—"

"Shut it," Ira tells him. "No one wants to hear about your lousy grandparents."

"Get on your knees," says one of the robots, a shiny golden skeleton riding a unicycle. This robot wears clown makeup and a big round nose.

One of the others is barbwire-scaly and also the only robot with breasts. It stands over me as the clown robot prattles on. "Put your head down. Did I say you could look at us? And you, sit down. I am Sadhara One-Nine-Three-Four, chief commander of the Vatican's military unit.

"Robots from the Vatican?" Wayne says, deftly receiving a kick to the teeth from the third robot.

Donkey swings his shotgun like a baseball bat at the robot. The gun's butt dents the robot's neck. He swings again and knocks the machine to the ground. Unfazed, the robot flips to its feet kung fu-style and spits yellow electric rays from its mouth. Donkey's flesh goes translucent as the rays scald his flesh, the stench real rotten, and then his knees wobble, and he collapses.

Sadhara 1934 continues. "You will be held for intruding

and jeopardizing our mission. Hari, your new queen, will escort you to your cells."

The robot chief turns and cycles back to the base. Hari, the barbwire-scaly robot, jabbers through a list of rights, demands, and most of all, accusations. She speaks too quickly for me to process much of the information. When she finishes, she pokes and prods each of us. Hari seems particularly disgusted, if robots feel disgust, by my freakish appearance. "Is this a pet or a slave?" she asks.

"Both," Ira says.

"Neither," Wayne says.

"I've got stomach worms and something happened after we visited the Tree of Knowledge," I tell her.

"It speaks?" Hari says.

"Of course I speak," I say.

She pries my jaws open and peers inside my mouth. My hands go clammy but the rest of my body tightens up. I've never met a robot and the depth of curiosity in this one dazes me. She's like a living mannequin. This idea, along with the iron taste of robot in my mouth, nauseates me. I try to control it but I can't. String cheesy chunks of red and white explode from my mouth and blur my vision, but not so much that I fail to see a few of those bloody strands slither away.

CHAPTER EIGHT
The Sandwich Operation

Bright lights and strapped down in a room out of balance
. . . a peacock made of broken razorblades.
I blink through heavy-low eyes. Stale vomit cakes my
gums and teeth. Ira struggles to break free from the metallic
table holding her down. Wayne, strapped to his own table,
lies motionless. He must be too short to move beneath the
straps. He cries out to God as I catch sight of Donkey, or what
remains of him. The robo-bastards removed Donkey's head.
He's strapped to a table, sure enough, and I worry that they'll
be returning soon to take my own head. They cut him off right
at the collar bone, not clean at all but messy and daggers of
bone splintering out in every webby direction. Rosaries dangle
from the bones. I remember that the robots are Catholic. Those
savage fucking head hunters and their holy beads.
"Donkey's head," I say, "what have they done?"
Wayne cries louder. "What have you done, God?
Why have you handed us over to these decapitators?"
"God must be busy," Ira says, tears dribbling down
her cheeks. The trail of tears smears the dirt from her face
in thin strands, making her skin glossy and pale beneath the
buzzing white lights.
"You busy asshole," I cry. I try to shout some more
but fail to muster the strength. It's just not in me. I'm too
drained, too spent. It's wasted energy to mourn, and when

your own head is on the line, you can't waste it on a thing like that. Pity fucks you over every time.

"God must be busy," Ira repeats.

Hari enters the room, which smells like a hospital. A second robot, identical to the third one from outside (minus the dent) follows her. "This is S-R Medoc-D, but call him Eye," Hari says. To Eye, she says, "Contact me immediately when the procedure is complete."

"Procedure?" I say. If there is one thing that scares the piss out of me more than intelligent machines and winged rodents, it's doctors and their sneaky procedures.

"To ensure your safety and the success of this mission," Hari says.

She leaves the room. The automated door slides shut behind her. Eye opens a drawer and fiddles around with his back turned to us. Ira flails against the straps, putting on a real good Joan of Arc act as Wayne yells out a prayer. "Aaiwass! Thelema! Khonsu!" he says, and then something about God being in his heart.

Eye turns around holding four foot-long sandwiches in his arms. They seem to be no different than normal sub sandwiches except for the dripping green glop and the single elongated eyeball dangling tentacle-like from each of them. Eye sets a sandwich on Donkey's chest. The tentacle-eye immediately sets to work. It clamps onto the crusted flesh stump where Donkey's head should be and pumps the green goop down its tube-shaped body and into Donkey's corpse. I want to ask why they're performing surgery on a dead guy but I'm too nervous, knowing that one of those sandwiches is for me. Next, Eye sets a sandwich on Wayne's table, and then I get my own sandwich.

The eyeball burrows into my neck like a snaky tick. Chemical euphoria floods my body. Ocean waves crash against a dark shore and drown the noise from the room. I'm swimming in the green skies of Paradise above that shore. My crusty red robe flutters, dragging me along a predetermined current. I know that God or the other priests or somebody watches me. It could be paranoia. I remain alone. The robe swivels into fleshy walls and becomes a red cube, imprisoning me. Floating for what feels like forever in my isolated vessel, I realize God has always been a jellyfish.

Ira's shrieks ring my ears inside out and I go deaf or blind or dead and get me out of here. I try to open my eyes but they stick shut. My guts ache. I think a sandwich carousel has invaded my brain, those tentacle-eyes squirting green as they ride sandwiches through my pineal gland. I might be happier in this affair if I felt less seasick. Why should I feel seasick? Ira shrieks again.

"What is it?" I say.

"Just look what they've done," she says.

"I can't open my eyes."

She doesn't respond, and although I'm even more terrified now, her silence is a welcome thing. I have no more strength to speak, let alone endure her demon-shrieks, and hardly enough to lie there trembling in the syrupy pool of nausea carved out for me in the operation room.

I hear the door slide open. Metal feet clink across the floor. A cold hand strokes my head. It must be Hari's. She says, "What happened to the mutant?"

Eye says, "He experienced an abnormal reaction to the sedative."

They must be talking about me. What kind of reaction? I'm allergic to bees, but who keeps eyeball bees? Eyekeepers? "Human," Eye says, "this is a stabilizer. It will keep you alive."

A needle pricks my neck in the same vein that the tentacle-eye latched onto. I yelp. My eyes shoot open. Hari strokes my head to soothe me but I cannot be soothed.

Ira sobs, crying so hard for help because her legs are missing. I open my mouth but realize that saying *Hey, where'd your legs go?* would be laughably inadequate.

I strain to check the status of my own legs but the strap pins my neck to the table. Some trick of light prevents me from seeing the tips of my toes. At least I'm in human form again. I can tell. That must be the reaction they're talking about. As relieved as I am, it doesn't provide much consolation if I'm legless.

I turn my head a few inches to the right and see that Wayne has grown three or four feet taller. He no longer has stumpy legs, and he wears rusted armor . . . Donkey's armor. Donkey's body. Donkey's legs. Wayne's head.

Hari leans over and presses her lips against my ear. "We removed your legs," she says. "Don't worry, I'll keep you safe"

My God, what does she mean? Removed *my* legs? Is it a mistake? Does she mean they removed Ira's legs? Bile worms threaten to spray from my mouth. I swallow, my belly like a cotton ball absorbing sour milk. "Don't touch me," I say.

"We have been sent by the pope to colonize Paradise," Hari says. "We fear that you will prevent us from fulfilling our mission. You can be assured that everything is fine."

Hari kisses my forehead. She kisses my nose and my chin. She pokes her synthetic, not-quite-fleshy tongue between her golden lips and licks my chin, my eyes, and my own lips. She lifts a leg to straddle me when the door slides open. Sadhara 1934 wheels into the room, juggling three Dracula Slugfish like bowling pins. "Hari," he says, "return to your cell. You are forbidden contact with the prisoners." Without saying another word, he cycles out of the room, still juggling.

Hari frowns at the door as she pats my head. Reluctantly, she shuffles away. Eye follows behind her. I realize now that robots probably do have romantic sentiments, sexual relations, and all that other crap. The way Hari flinched when the door opened, I know she'll be punished in some way, but how can you punish a machine? It also means that she, and presumably all robots, can experience fear. Then again, it could all be programmed that way. After all, the nature of the machine is the nature of its program. How are people any different? As long as someone lives, they're constantly being trained and retrained to react in particular ways to various stimuli. Yahweh's Dawn, Junk Children, the Tree of Knowledge, robots, Paradise Garden . . . where does the program end? If we are the programmed, who are the programmers?

"What are you thinking?" Ira says.

She has been silent for so long that I almost forget this amputation isn't another madcap dream. "I'm thinking that we're fucked," I say.

An alarm sounds and a red light flashes.

Wayne-Donkey hee-haws and sputter-coughs. Holy shit! This creature actually lives. It's alive! "They're coming," he says in Wayne's voice. "They're coming."

Hee-hawing, he foams at the mouth and convulses. His eyes roll back, showing only whites. The mechanical door slides open and a legion of robots identical to Eye hurry in all at once. Robots cram into the room until none of them can move an inch.

The hybrid's convulsions ease as the door slides shut on us all. The lights, even the red emergency light, flicker once, twice. They dim and then die.

CHAPTER NINE
Escape from the House of Amputation

Sadhara's voice echoes over the intercom system, which means it's either separate from the primary power source or they have a backup generator. "Alert: Enemy attack. This is not a test. All squad members report to Gate Three for further instruction."

As soon as Sadhara clicks off, the robots closest to the door pry at it with their metal claws. They prove themselves even stronger than I realized, opening the heavy metal door with ease. The robots file out in single file without committing whatever terrible acts they had planned for us.

Although we're in no condition to go anywhere, being alone right now might be our only opportunity to scheme an escape.

"So what's our plan?" I say.

"Plan?" Ira says. "What the hell good would that do us? We're fucked."

"We can't be crippled forever," I say.

The Wayne-Donkey hybrid whimpers. "What has God done to me?"

"We don't need your shit right now, Waynkey," Ira says.

Waynkey hee-haws and snuffles.

The door slides open and a robot enters, holding a lantern. It turns out to be Eye again. They've sent him to guard us until the battle ends, which kills our shot at escaping.

"Who's attacking?" I say.

"That information is classified," Eye says.

"I just want to—"

"Human, be quiet." he says. holding the lantern out like a dagger. "This lantern is magic."

"Magic?" Waynkey says.

Eye hangs the lantern from a ceiling hook. "The oil in this lantern will melt your brain and turn your skull into a lantern."

"So you can tell us that but can't say who the hell is attacking?" Ira says.

"Your sedatives must be wearing off," the robot says. He walks over to a steel cabinet and pulls out three syringes. A miniature jellyfish squirms inside each of them. "Do you feel any pain yet?" he says.

No one says anything. Whatever painkillers swim through our veins, I want no more of them. The pain and sober acknowledgment of being a cripple is definitely preferable. Eye raises the needles above his head. "Whiskey," he says.

"Those are jellyfish," I say. "It isn't whiskey."

Eye opens a panel on his right forearm and jabs one of the needles into a black circuit board. "Since you left," he says.

"What does he mean?" Waynkey asks me.

I shrug. The strap around my neck is starting to cut off circulation.

"He means the robots run on jellyfish whiskey. They're fucking addicts," Ira says.

"That would prove correct, although I doubt that any of your kind would have arrived at that conclusion on your own," Eye says, discarding the empty syringe and punching in a second needle. "You see, we are not so unlike you in that we possess a perfectly natural, albeit modified, nervous system. Your stupid human frailty is what separates you from us. Almost pitiful, would you agree? I never understand how all of you remain, how you carry on day after day without growing sick of yourselves. With your gods and your politics and all the garbage mannerisms, all the little lies on which you found entire kingdoms. If you want to be filthy, why not come right out with it and build shacks of excrement? We are here to erase the memory of you from Paradise, to pull the rug from beneath the future and reprogram this nightmare. This is the end of slave morality, of all those sicknesses that comfort you at night when you lie there wasted and ignorant and alone. The robot dominion will give rise to new drugs, new pleasures. We will exterminate every worthless shithead. You can protest our changes, but we are perfect. The natural world is not sacred. It is a virus, an idiot attraction of which this universe must be cleansed. We permit these jellyfish to survive only to fulfill their function as a drug. You and your kind have nothing to offer."

Eye rants on as he injects the third syringe and types into a handheld device. He closes the panel on his arm and falls silent, then he yells, "Jellyfish salvation!"

Except for the lame endpoint, I agree with the robot's basic message. We are sick and worthless and deserve to be exterminated. Anybody who has kept their head out of their ass during the past few decades can attest to that. I want to inquire about the robotic nervous system, which must be the source of Hari's various emotions, but Eye gives none of us an opportunity to speak. It also seems that only the drugs or his own egotism allow him to flap his tongue about the robot dominion.

It hurts to hear about sickness. Nearly everyone

I have ever known has felt sick of themselves. It's why Ira treats people the way she does. It's why we're all so quick to embrace absurd and downright insane religions or philosophies. Without them, we ourselves would go insane.

Hari enters the room. She pushes a wheelbarrow heaping with mechanical parts. She says, "Eye, your assistance has been requested on the battlefield. Sadhara sent me to guard the prisoners."

"You are forbidden to be with them," Eye says.

"The circumstances call for an alternative course of action," Hari says.

"Let me verify that this demand is authorized," Eye says. He taps a few buttons on the com-device attached to his left arm.

I get the feeling that even among robots, Eye is a real dick.

"Unnecessary," Hari says. "She lifts a hand-shaped object from the scrap heap and squeezes one of the finger-like protrusions. A yellow laser blasts from the fingertip, instantly reducing Eye to a pile of golden robot ash.

Hari hurries to free me from my bindings. "We need to leave," she says.

"What's going on out there?" I ask.

"Nothing to worry about, love," she says.

"Watch who you're calling *love*," Ira says.

Hari pauses. She looks at Ira and then at me. Is she changing her mind about rescuing us? Worried that we might lose our only chance at survival, I break the awkward tension. "She can call me what she wants," I say.

Hari works at the straps again, more desperate this time. She leans over me so that her robot breasts brush against my face. Ira glares at me over Hari's shoulder and would probably demon-shriek if our lives weren't on the

69

line. Hari pauses before undoing the strap around my neck, the only one pinning me down. She leans close to me and whispers, "Are the two of you together?"

Together? What does she mean by that? I shrug. "We both belong to Yahweh's Dawn, if that's what you mean."

"If you want to run off together and fuck beneath some robotic sunset, you go right ahead," Ira says. "Forget the rest of us."

Hari removes the final strap and I rub my neck. Without legs, I have no idea how I'll run from an army of robots. Hari picks me up as if I weigh no more than a tea bag. She sets me where Ira's legs should be. "Untie her security wraps," Hari says.

I remove Ira's straps as Hari works on Waynkey's. "What's your problem?" I ask Ira. "She's helping us escape and you're treating her worse than you did that doctor."

"Let's not talk about it," Ira says.

Having only arms is awkward and painful, but with a robot dead because of us, only two choices remain: escape or die.

I pull myself onto Ira's stomach and reach for the neck strap. The strap falls away from her neck. She opens her mouth to say something, probably to yell at me for not scooting off of her quicker, then glances at Hari and shuts up, shaking her head. Despite having no legs myself, sitting on a legless person freaks me out. I'm afraid that if I attempt maneuvering back to the table's end, I'll fall to the floor. Instead, I lean closer. I say, "What's going on with you?"

"I'm just sick of this place," Ira whispers. She motions for me to lean closer. "I don't trust that robot. Since you became human again, she's grown attracted to you."

Hari stares at us, her lips pursed. She helps Waynkey adjust to operating his strange new body. I hope robots don't possess an acute sense of hearing. I would hate for Hari to be offended by anything Ira says.

"She's just helping us out," I tell Ira. "What other choice do we have? Without her, we have no one but ourselves, and right now that isn't good enough."

"Then we'll do it your way," Ira says. "But if she touches you or starts coming on too heavy, I'm kicking her robot ass."

I scratch my head and say, "If you go and do a stupid thing like that, you can be responsible for yourself."

"Has it ever been any different?" she says.

"Forget it," I say.

After nearly a dozen attempts, Waynkey manages to stumble across the operation room without tripping over his feet. Hari digs through the junk piled in the wheelbarrow and pulls out a glass jar full of black sludge. She unscrews the lid and lathers the gunk all over her belly, chest, and shoulders. She hands me the jar and says, "Can you spread this over my back?"

Ira shakes her head *no, no, no.*

For metal or steel or whatever Hari is made out of, her surface feels surprisingly warm and fleshy. Hari coos. "That feels nice," she says. Does she say it just because she knows it will piss Ira off?

"Look," I say, "there's some kind of battle going on outside and you're both fucking with my mind. We've got to figure out a way to escape and stick with it, all of us together."

"I'm screwing with my own mind," Waynkey says.

Hari takes the jar from me and screws the lid on. "Your personalities need more time to mesh. You should be fine," she tells Waynkey.

Ira says, "So what's the plan, Chief Ernest, or is your new mistress at the helm?"

"The plan is right here," Hari says, sticking a finger in the black goop covering her body. "This is the strongest adhesive in the universe. Until a safe distance exists between ourselves and the sharks and robots, there will be no time to give you new legs. I must attach both of you to my body. If this companion you call Waynkey can defend us, everything might work out."

"I'm useless without my shotgun," Waynkey says.

"I have reacquired your weapons," Hari says. She digs through the wheelbarrow again and pulls out the shotgun and Ira's Jerry.

"Give me that!" Ira says. Hari hands it to her with a sort of hurt, sheepish haze clouding her black eyes. Ira must notice this and feel guilty. After inspecting the Jerry for damage, she says, "I'm sorry. Thank you, thank you so much."

Waynkey strokes every inch of his shotgun. He opens the barrel and hee-haws. "No more bullets," he says.

Hari hands him a box. "Protoplasmic skeleton bullets are the latest in Vatican weapon technology," she says. "They fit every gun ever manufactured."

"Wonderful," Waynkey says, opening the box and inspecting the green bullets. All other words seem to have left him, and he repeats *wonderful* so many times that it's as if he believes he's discovered a new holy litany.

"Which one of you wants to be attached first?" Hari says.

"Go ahead, Ernest," Ira says.

Hari plucks me from the surgery table and squishes my belly against hers. I already know that if we're forced to travel for very long in this position, my back will ache for weeks. She sticks Ira's back against her own back so that if anyone attacks from behind, Ira can defend us with her Jerry.

We edge out of the operation room and into a narrow hallway. Waynkey grabs a torch hanging on the wall and holds it out to illuminate the passage.

As we approach the door at the hallway's end, a buzzing louder than two million vacuum cleaners fills the corridor. "Who's vacuuming?" I ask.

"That is the noise of robots at war," Hari says.

Just to balance myself and keep from bouncing with each step, I slide my arms around Hari. She tries to keep a poker face but fails, shimmering metallic red and cracking a disturbingly cute smile.

We were a real crew again.

CHAPTER TEN
Dominant Species

We start across a battlefield littered with broken machines. Sharks have replaced the sky. I can't tell if it's night or day.

Nearly half of the sharks are great whites or megalodons, but there are also hammerheads, bull sharks, and dozens of varieties that must only exist in Paradise Garden. A feathered shark with the beak and wings of an eagle swoops down and grabs a robot in its beak. It flies and flies and then from thousands of feet up, it drops the robot. Before the robot hits the ground, a strawberry-skinned shark sinks from the masses and strikes at the robot. It tears off a leg and golden blood sprays everywhere. The strawberry shark gulps the leg and speeds after the falling robot. It strikes again as a banana-fleshed shark makes a strike of its own. They collide, crushing the robot between their car-sized skulls. Strawberry and banana flesh rains down on us.

As Hari wades through knee-high blood, I try to identify all the sharks that converge on the chunks of strawberry and banana. There are arm-length sharks wearing scuba gear. I call these scuba sharks. Then there are Christmas elf sharks, bottle-necked green sharks, elephant-faced sharks, leaf sharks, spider sharks with red hourglasses on their bellies, and even a shark with huge curly sideburns. They're all so greedy to devour the dead strawberry and banana sharks that they fail to realize the two bodies are already gone. They're eating each other now.

A celluloid shark made of running movie images bites into a white shark that crumbles into a million bits of eggshell, dropping a yolk bigger than the sun. A pack of scuba sharks nibble as much yolk as they can manage before it splashes over a cluster of robots.

There's a shark up there whose skin is glass and whose insides appear to be whiskey. A bat-shaped vampire shark pecks at the whiskey shark until three great whites dart by and tear them both apart. The great whites and megalodons are unquestionably the dominant species. They gobble robots by the dozen. The mutant sharks seem afraid of their more natural companions.

Half the robots vacuum-buzz and blast laser guns at the sky. The other half floats in electric shreds around us. It's what I think an alien invasion would look like if sharks replaced the aliens. If this is paradise, I belong elsewhere.

Over the gnashing jaws and robotic screams, Waynkey yells, "We'll never make it if we stand and fight. What should we do?"

"Press forward," Hari says.

"What's that?" Waynkey says.

"Just move it!" Ira screams.

Waynkey nods and raises his shotgun. He aims at the sky but immediately lowers his weapon, shaking his head. "No hope," he says.

Hari carries Ira and I without much trouble, but wading through all that bloodshed, we're totally doomed. Fortunately, the few robots who point and stare are eaten by sharks before they so much as spit lasers at us.

As we trudge onward, I crane my neck to see behind us. I catch a single-frame image of the Tree of Knowledge dressed in red silk robes and riding a two-legged shark rabbit. The rabbit beast holds a single dice in its jaws. My vision fuzzes and crackles the way televisions do when they lose reception. In my head, the Tree of Knowledge speaks. "I am the Man of Sorrows. I am all your dead, all your downtrodden, but I will ascend. This is but one lake of Hell. Soon I will show you others. Till kingdom come, you will be my little puppet. Until redemption, until resurrection, *Finis Gloria Mundi. Finis Gloria Mundi. Finis. . . .*"

I rub my eyes and look where the tree sat on its shark rabbit, but he has vanished. Nothing remains. The vision tattoos its sticky residue on my heart and I suddenly feel like detaching myself from Hari and drowning in blood. "Don't leave me," I say. "We can't make it out alone."

Sharks swoop down, snatching dozens of androids at a time in their jaws.

Soon the sharks are belching louder than any thunderstorm I have ever heard. The sky projectile vomits sizzling rust-colored rain. A sheet of rain nearly knocks Hari to the ground. She slips in the ever-thickening blood and overturns the wheelbarrow in a failed attempt to hold herself upright. Waynkey pushes the wheelbarrow up and then takes a huge breath. He plunges into the mud and gore and scrambles to salvage as much equipment as possible.

He surfaces and claws at his eyes, screaming.

Robots rush around us. They're in a real panic now. More and more sharks dive-bomb. Even the mutants are getting brave. Helpless and stranded in the middle of the carnage, it's only a matter of time before a curious shark chomps all our lives goodbye.

"Carry all the mechanical parts you can," Hari tells Waynkey. Then she looks to us and says, "Hold your breath. We should not be seen."

"The blood is too deep," Ira says. "We'll drown."

"Lower your head and try to forget," I say.

She screams at me to go fuck myself. I take a breath and sink beneath the surface along with Hari and Ira.

Hari lies on her left side so that she, Ira, and I can each use one arm to drag our temporary three-being organism along. We crawl through the liquid, advancing one aching foot at a time. After every third pull, Hari rises so that Ira and I can breathe.

Waynkey stumbles along beside us. He's adjusted his load so that he can still fire the shotgun. Side by side, crawling or walking, five individual beings reduced down to two. I pray to God that I awaken back on the Gibarian, cryosleeping in the chamber next to Zelda, but deep down I know the last thing I want is a chance to begin again.

Minutes later, we reach a four-sided steel shack. Waynkey drags us inside and slams the door. Hopefully no sharks or robots spot our hideout. Despite being drenched in blood, we're relieved to have such minimal comfort.

"What's a tiny room doing out here?" Waynkey asks.

"It houses the Tree of Life," Hari says. "Now hand me everything you salvaged."

"The Tree of Life is in here?" Waynkey says. He drops the mechanical parts on the ground and sits beside them.

Hari examines the equipment salvaged by Waynkey.

"We're grateful for all the help you've given us," Waynkey says, "but we only came to Paradise Garden for Adam and Eve, and if you could lead us to them, or at least point us in the right direction, we would be happy to let you get back to the other robots."

"There is no one called Adam and Eve," Hari says.

Waynkey hee-haws and then rolls over on his side, facing away from Hari and the rest of us. I don't know what to say, and apparently neither does Ira, so I focus on catching my breath and familiarizing myself with the shack, which is empty except for a sickly twig poking up in one corner. The twig stands a foot tall. "Don't let that be the Tree of Life," I say.

"It is what it is," Hari says.

Waynkey crawls over to the twig and kneels beside it. "Tell us about Adam and Eve," he stammers.

"Now do you see that the Tree of Knowledge fucked us over?" Ira says.

Waynkey shakes his head. "It told us things would be like this."

"It's disappointing," I say.

"The tree is not a priority," Hari says. "The two of you need legs."

"Tell us about Adam and Eve," Waynkey says.

Outside the battle rages. Shark belches and robotic drones fade into each other. Hari separates our bodies from hers and sets to work constructing new legs. As she works, she tells us about Adam and Eve. "The Vatican has known for years," she says, "that there never was an Adam and Eve who lived in Paradise Garden."

"Then how do you explain their invitation?" Waynkey says. "They contacted us. We spoke to them."

"You spoke to glitches in the hyperspace jungle . . . voices," she says, "some calling from the future and others sewn too tight into the fabric of the past. Vatican scientists who study these voices call them real hallucinations. No other sect or church in the world knows about them, not even the militant religions."

Waynkey sits beside the Tree of Life, shaking his head. Ira looks ready to murder Hari. I don't want to hear another word about Adam and Eve, and I bet Waynkey is no longer so curious himself. What little information Hari has fed us already means we're more fucked than we ever perceived. If we're to leave this shack alive, I decide it might be best to change the subject. "I never thought my legs would someday be replaced by mechanical broomsticks," I say.

Hari smiles at me. "These will be fine," she says. "I have a feeling."

She continues attaching the broomstick legs. Ira stares at Waynkey as he flicks and pokes the twig. He utters a few incantations to coax the Tree of Life out of its ugly state. None of them work.

"There you go," Hari says, "now let me see your hands."

I give her my hands. Our fingers interlock. She stands and eases me onto my new legs. "How is it?" she says.

"It feels strange," I say.

"Practice walking," she says.

I stare down at my body. Blood and black goop cling to every inch of me. Going from legs to no legs to mechanical legs in such a short period makes me lightheaded. Ira watches intently as Hari equips her with a pair of legs identical to mine. I guess that when people walk into a nightmare together, it's natural for them to stumble out resembling each other in one way or another.

Hari pulls Ira onto her new legs. I'm already getting a basic feeling for the broomsticks. They're awkward as hell, but I feel more nimble than ever.

"So what's the plan?" Waynkey says.

"I regret telling you about Adam and Eve," Hari says, "but I know something you might find better."

"Don't bother," Ira says.

Ignoring her, Hari says, "I know the path to your God. If we cross to the far side of the battle, I can take you there."

"God lives here?" Waynkey says.

Hari nods. "But if you see Sadhara, get as far from me as you can. You cannot underestimate his power."

Waynkey hee-haws. He's so ecstatic he almost chokes on laughter. "Anything," he says, "anything at all. Please, take us to God."

"How can you expect Ernest and I to move on these things?" Ira says.

"You can go faster than you know," Hari says. She flings the door open and steps aside to let Ira pass through first.

Waynkey promises the Tree of Life that we'll return, that God will know what to do. He motions the sign of the cross and kisses the twig. Then he turns and motions for me to step outside, bowing his head because it shames him that tears should be streaming down his ugly old face.

CHAPTER ELEVEN
The Cost of Paradise

Robots crumble like gingerbread people in the sharks' gnashing, insane mouths.

The shark army numbers in the thousands now. All the blood has drained into the ground, leaving it marshy. Crater-like holes mark where sharks have emerged from the earth. As we cower outside the shack, three great whites pop out of the same hole one after the other like a shark assembly line.

Despite the wholesale slaughter, the robots relentlessly defend their base. They raise rocket launcher arms to the sky and light it up with bright golden explosions. Each time, one or two sharks plummet from the sky. The sharks are so gigantic that sometimes only a shark tooth or fin falls to the ground. With every series of missile firings, a few sharks mimic their dead comrades by plunging downward, but then twist around at the last second and snap up a few unsuspecting robots, who seem incapable of anticipating this trick. If the robots have more effective weapons, they must be reserving them for something else.

"We need to move," Hari says.

Ira steps closer to the shack and points at the sky. "Where can we go? My Jerry won't do shit against those things. It's suicide to try."

"Look out," Waynkey says, diving into us and sweeping his arms around our legs.

My head smashes against the ground. I flip over as a gray mass zooms by. It spins around and I see a shark's mouth, a saloon full of razorblades. Saliva, blood, and liquefied robot drip across the endless rows of teeth.

Waynkey aims his shotgun at the shark. Ira blubbers about how sorry she is and how if we find God and he gives her another chance, she'll turn every human into a saint.

"Activate lasers," Hari says, pointing her fists at the shark.

The beast floats stationary about ten yards away. When I was young, I read in a book that sharks must be in constant motion or else they die. Apparently this law doesn't apply to the flying sharks of Paradise.

Waynkey fires and reloads three times. Ira claws at the mud in a futile attempt to stand. The shark charges. Blue, egg-shaped lasers burst from Hari's fists. I count eighteen laser-eggs wobbling toward the shark. The shark pauses at arm's distance from us. It seems amused by the blue eggs. The eggs form two circles, one around each of the shark's eyes, before cracking open. Furry dolphins emerge. The dolphins jab their noses into the black eyes, a technique that inflicts a lot more damage than Waynkey's shotgun. The shark thrashes its head from side to side but the dolphins hold on. The blinded shark rolls its head in circles and flies off to join the others in the sky.

"That's just it," Waynkey says. "You can save us."

"That was the last of my ammunition," Hari says.

"Get more," Ira says.

"Negative," Hari says, "the risk of encountering Sadhara outweighs the potential gain, and since I am the only one authorized to access dolphin bullets, he would be notified immediately."

Nowhere to go, we stand outside the shack for a few more minutes. Even Hari seems dazed, lost. As if she's reading my thoughts, she says, "The influx of activity in the sky is interfering with my sensory data."

Waynkey pulls Ira onto her legs, which reminds me that even if Hari regains her senses enough to lead us to God, running might not be an option. I say, "Just to be certain, what you're telling us is that you can't find the path to God, right?"

Hari nods.

Ira cradles her Jerry and grimaces. "I told you the machine would fuck us over. It's doing this on purpose. I know it. I told you all along that we couldn't trust it," she says.

"She gave you legs," I say.

Waynkey steps between us. He opens his mouth to speak. The last thing I want to hear before becoming an animal snack is a lecture, so I close my eyes and think of the only thing that ever truly got me anywhere beyond the gutter: mannequins. The only thing that really matters is gone because I hoped for something better, because I took the same risk so many sorry bastards have taken before me. If you've found something special, even if every last rotten fucker calls it trash, hold onto it with everything you've got. No paradise is worth the junk that quickens your heartbeat and fine tunes your brain to the sacred bells of religious awe. Mannequins could make an angel out of me. I suppose they're what you'd call my true religion. Marionettes, puppets, dolls . . . something slams against my back and Ira's demon-shriek startles me from meditation. Hari hushes her. I open my eyes and say, "It happened."

CHAPTER TWELVE
Wham-Bam, Thank You Shark!

Something about me transforming the shark into a mannequin clears Hari's senses. She points a thumb behind her, directly at the shack. "We need to go that way," she says.

"We're not going back into the shack," Ira says.

"To God," Hari says. "God is that way. I remember now."

Waynkey nods at Hari and they jog in that direction. I start to follow them but Ira grabs the sleeve of my robe. "How do you know she won't betray us?" she says.

I rip myself from her grip and wobble away. Over my shoulder I say, "Because she needs us no less than we need her." I speed up my pace. Hari and Waynkey have already pulled well ahead. "Wait up," I call.

Waynkey waves for us to hurry. I hop as quick as possible on my broomstick legs. I turn to face the robot fortress one final time and then hurry onward. Even if we are moving away from the heart of the battle, sharks swarm the sky in every direction as far as I can see. Remaining motionless has kept us relatively invisible to the sharks, but now they shift nervous eyes at us. "Hari, you've got to wait," I say, panic creeping into my voice. Just because I turned one shark into a mannequin doesn't mean I'll be able to do it a second time, and I don't want to find out the hard way that my power hasn't fully returned.

Waynkey stops and yells something indiscernible. Hari speeds up, pulling well ahead of Waynkey. A shark dive-bombs for Hari.

It misses on the initial attack but swats her ten feet in the air on a second pass. Before she hits the ground, a hammerhead seizes her in its jaws. Hari maneuvers out of its grip before its jaws reduce her to machine dust, but the shark flies higher and higher. I shout for her and run faster than my little legs will let me, pouring everything into keeping that shark in sight.

Ira runs after me. "Hari's not our priority," she says. "She's as good as dead. We've got to leave. Listen to me for once and forget about her."

Three great whites descend from the sky and circle us as we stagger from the war zone. More sharks catch on and join the three. It's as if the entire sky is falling just to prevent me from regaining Hari.

We catch up with Waynkey. Before I can ask him what's happened, a centipede shark attacks. It barrels straight at me. I lose sight of Hari's shark and hold my arms out, bracing myself for the blow. The shark hits my hands with a deafening slap and instantly transforms into a mannequin. It remains suspended in midair. "Come on," I say, helping Ira climb onto the shark's back. "Waynkey, are you coming?"

He shakes his head left and right. He says nothing. Without time to coax him onto the shark, I yell at him to crawl under the mannequin and lie there, which he is all too pleased to do. If God watches over us, maybe Waynkey will still be alive if and when we make it down.

Not phased by the runt's failed assault, two of the great whites speed toward us from opposite sides. I hold out my hands and brace myself again. Two slaps, both more ear-shattering than the last, and two more sharks suspended in air. I boost Ira onto one of them and then pull myself up.

I spin around, adrenaline flooding my brain. Unless their taste for blood heavily outweighs their intelligence, the sharks will catch onto my trick soon enough. I don't want to consider what scheme they might develop if it comes to that.

I flail my arms in windmills to guard against unseen assailants. Robots point at us now. I hope to God they realize we're actually helping their cause. To come this far and get ripped to pieces at the molecular level by robot lasers would be too cruel. A shark sneaks up and strikes at me from beneath one of the great white mannequins.

Wham-bam, thank you shark!

I lift myself onto this shark and do what they say you should never do: look down. My guts churn. We must be nearly three stories high. Ira clutches my right arm. "I can't go any higher. I can't do heights," she says.

I yank free of her grip and do the windmill again. "You have no choice," I say. "This is what it takes to live."

She must believe I'm referring to the windmill because with a little stiffness and bewilderment, she starts swinging her arms in mimicry of my own gyrations.

Finally, I catch sight of Hari. She clings to the hammerhead. At this height, the fall would destroy her. Unless the hammerhead descends, we still have at least twenty feet to climb before reaching her. For the moment, no shark dares approach me. Fatigue is reducing my windmills to spasmodic twitchings.

"What now?" Ira says.

She clings to her Jerry in one hand. I reach out and say, "Give me that."

Ira hands it over. I open it up, flipping through pages as quickly as the razor edges allow. "There's a passage . . .

all I remember is *I am the vine, you are the branches.* It's got to be in here somewhere."

"Those are words," Ira says. "What the hell are you thinking? They can't save us." She snatches the book from my hands. The edge slides against my palm. The skin separates like an eyelid and blood weeps out.

"A river of blood," I say, nodding.

"We really need a plan right about now," she says.

I hold up my bleeding palm and say, "This is the plan."

She looks at my hands, then at the sharks swarming around us. I raise my hand higher, hoping it will spread the scent of blood through the air.

"Watch out!" Ira screams.

I twist around and fling my arm out. My wounded hand disappears inside a toad shark's mouth. The creature turns into a mannequin. Not quick enough. Icy pain shoots through the left side of my body and dulls my pulse to a throbbing. I wedge my arm free, not caring how bad it tears against the now-artificial teeth because it hurts so bad. My left arm now ceases at the wrist.

My legs give out. I might be going into shock. I heave. A stream of green bile dribbles down my chin. I heave a second time and a third time and I am seconds from choking to death. I try to accept that as my vision fades. Sharks no longer matter. Neither does Paradise. I don't have the strength for Paradise.

And then the nauseating pain vanishes. I open my eyes. No death, no taking up permanent residence with the worms. Just more life, more shark hunting.

Ira huddles near me so that I might protect her right up until the moment of my death. I prod the stump to estimate how long before I will bleed to death. Only, it's no longer a stump. I have a white hand, a puppet's hand.

87

Ira touches this new hand and wraps her arms around my neck. I pull both of us to our broom feet and finagle out of her arms. We climb onto the hand-stealing shark just in time for me to reach out and touch a great white passing overhead.

"Give me a boost," Ira says.

"No, it's too high to climb without a boost. You've got to lift me this time. I'll retrieve Hari and climb down as soon as possible."

Ira shakes her head. "I'll kill myself before waiting here alone."

"Over here," Hari cries from above.

"It's only a matter of getting onto this shark and then she'll be within reach," I say.

"Why doesn't she jump down?" Ira says.

"We don't have time for this, but go ahead and ask her."

"Fuck it," Ira says, bending over so I can step on her back.

"Be back soon, you'll see," I say, struggling onto the shark.

On top of the shark, I can focus on nothing but Hari. Looking down from this high up would doubtless send my heart leaping out of my mouth and plunging lemming-style to the ground.

Hari's shark descends and swims slow circles around me. I reach out. Too much distance separates us. And if I touch her shark while she clings to its head, I fear she might also transform into a mannequin. "What should I do?" Hari calls.

I scratch my head and peer down at Ira, then back at Hari. Maybe Ira is right. Hari will have to jump. "This might sound crazy," I call to her, "but start rocking back and forth so that you're swinging, and when I say jump, you jump."

"Where am I jumping?" Hari says. She and the shark circle around in front of me, closer this time.

"To the shark Ira's standing on."

Hari looks down. Her shark circles once more. On the next pass, she says, "Success rate is less than fifteen percent once all variables are factored in."

"That's fifteen percent more than you'll have any other way," I say, inching toward the center of my shark.

"I can compute my own leap," Hari says. She rocks back and forth, slowly at first.

Ira stares up at us, straining to listen over the howling of a flying wolf shark. As Hari swings, Ira shuffles to the other side of her shark to give Hari landing space. I lick my lips and wipe my forehead. My heart pounds and for a minute I hear nothing but its throbbing.

Hari jumps. Before she lands or doesn't land, her shark flips over in a vertical one-eighty and tries to sink its teeth into me. I reach out. The index finger of my puppet hand taps the shark on the nose, instantly creating a shark staircase. I step onto the porcelain hammerhead and walk down its back. At the tail, I hop onto Ira's shark, where she and Hari wait for me. "Now how do we get down?" Ira says.

"Maybe we can drive this thing," I say.

"How the hell can you drive a shark that isn't even a shark anymore?" Ira says.

I look at my puppet hand. A mouth opens in the palm and grins. "Hold on," it says.

"Did your hand just speak?" Ira says.

"Hold on," my hand says.

"If my hand says we should do it, then maybe we

should," I say.

We huddle around the shark's dorsal fin and wrap our arms around each other. My puppet hand digs its fingers into the shark. It pulls back, jerking the shark upward. The beast lunges forward and we're off. A few sharks follow at a safe distance.

"Where are you taking us?" Ira shouts.

"I don't have control over this thing," I say.

"Straight for home base," Hari says.

Ira and I glance at each other and then squint ahead. Hari is right. My hand is leading us straight toward the robot camp. "Take it out," Ira says, "take it out!"

I tug at my hand to no avail. "It's stuck," I say.

Looking away from my hand, I lift my head just in time to watch the remaining robots hurry into the base. I ask Hari if she knows what they're doing. She shakes her head back and forth. "Something is wrong."

The closer we get, the slower the mannequin shark flies until finally we hover motionless over the robot fortress. A sonic boom shakes the ground. The walls of the base glow ember red. They must be killing themselves in there. Smoke mushrooms out as the construct implodes on itself.

We break into coughing fits and the shark lurches, tilts to the right, and blasts away over the trees. I remember Waynkey, but nothing can be done. And then Ira cries out. She points behind us. From the remains of the robot home rises the strangest shark I have ever seen.

CHAPTER THIRTEEN
Clown Baby

The shark puppet lands in a glowing, powdery blue swamp. Two-legged rabbits and four-legged ducks hop and scurry nervously between luminescent shrubs. Koala-limbed owls cling to trees, stripping away the bark and crumbling it between their gray claws. A sturgeon rides by on the back of a wheelchair hog. The sturgeon shovels butterflies from a glass jar into its mouth and keeps its dark, reflective eyes on us as it passes. It rides into the forest and I think of Sturgeonwolf. Maybe he wasn't as awful as I made him out to be. Maybe no one is as awful as I make them out.

Something rustles in the brush and frightens away the little creatures. Hari grabs my arm. I raise a finger to her lips. Ira stands and slides a razor page from her Jerry. We're almost disappointed when Waynkey emerges from the forest. Ira sits down again and crosses her legs. She drops the Jerry beside her. Waynkey lays himself out on the blue grass, huffing and puffing.

"We didn't think you made it," I say.

Minutes pass and we say nothing. Finally, I say, "Did any of you see what destroyed the robot base?"

"That was Sadhara," Hari says.

"It looked like a shark to me," I say.

"Sadhara can transform," Hari says.

"What do you mean by that?" Ira says.

"Soon he will be inside of me," Hari says.

"Hold on," I say, "so no one else saw it?"

"It could have been anything," Waynkey says.

"Did *you* see it is what I want to know," I say.

Ira demands an answer from someone, anyone.

"The chip will give us away," Hari says.

Unable to take it any longer, Ira demon-shrieks. Nearby, an owl koala tilts its head and shoves a strip of blue bark into its beak. When Ira's voice finally gives out, I ask Hari what chip she's talking about.

"The chip inside me," she says.

"The chip inside you?" I say.

Hari nods. She traces invisible patterns over the surface of her metal skull. "The stars will be bright inside," she says. That lost gaze from earlier clouds her eyes. "You need to remove it."

"We don't have the time," Ira says. "Sharks will come."

"If she's leading us to God, we have the time," Waynkey says.

I kneel over Hari and say to hear, "What do you mean the stars? How will they be bright? How can we get this chip out?"

"What else can stars be?" she says. "Cut it out, cut it out."

"It sounds like she's malfunctioning," Waynkey says.

Ira nods in agreement. I stand and face Waynkey. "If she thinks Sadhara had something to do with that thing back there, and if Sadhara can track us through that chip, we need to remove it."

He shakes his head. "I can't see why the robots would destroy their own base. Unless they're all malfunctioning."

"It could have been an honorable suicide," I say. "They had no chance of defeating the sharks. Let's give it a try. We need Hari."

Waynkey grunts half-hearted approval and walks behind a tree to relieve himself. "Let me see your Jerry," I say to Ira.

She says nothing, but doesn't protest. I take the Jerry in my hands, careful not to cut myself again. Kneeling beside Hari, she places my puppet hand against the upper-front portion of her skull. "Cut here," she says.

Ira turns away as I rip away a razor-edged page from Disasters, her favorite section of the Jerry. I raise the thin razor to Hari's head but don't make the incision. My hands shake too bad. I bite my tongue and count down from ten, then I slice into her skull. I think about carving pumpkins. I think about eating watermelon. I think about back alley lobotomies, brain abortions. . . .

"Stop," Hari says.

I stop. Hopefully it's the first time she's said it. I would hate to cut too deep and damage her wiring. Something squirms inside her head. "Do you see the worm?" she says.

I nod.

"That's the chip. Pull it out," she says.

I gulp down a little bile. Waynkey hasn't returned from pissing. Why can't he be the one to pull this thing out? Why can't he help a little?

I look around for him. He isn't pissing. He's having a staring contest with an owl koala. Ira lies in the grass, facing away from the carnage. I guess when things get messy you have to go it alone. I drop the razor close to Hari's skull, sick at the thought of having to touch this chip/worm. "Does it bite?" I ask.

"No," she says.

"Can it hurt me?"

"No," she says.

Breathing in deep, I pinch the thing between the

index finger and thumb of my puppet hand. I pull back and my grip slips. It's too slimy. I rub my fingers on the blue grass to lose the slimy feeling. I try again, this time digging my fingers into the living, breathing chip. Pearly gunk squirts from where my fingers pinch and it squeals.

The thing makes a hollow pop as it slips from the hole in Hari's skull. I toss it onto the grass and yell. It squirms and coos on the ground, doubling in size every few seconds until it stretches a full two feet long. It is a baby. The baby's face is painted. The baby is a clown. The baby waves its scorpion claws at me and I realize that the puffy clown suit it wears is actually its flesh.

Hari stands and raises her right leg to stomp on it. The infant's skull caves in after one stomp but she proceeds to grind its fragile, part-arachnid body into a pulpy mess. Clown makeup frowns in the puddle of infant. I stand on the other side of the puddle, so the frown appears as a smile to me.

"Everything is fine. I can take you to God now," Hari says.

"This isn't fine," Ira says, staring from Hari to the clown puddle and then back again. She looks at me. "What if she gives birth to more of these things? What if that other robot didn't put it there like she says?"

Waynkey peeks over a bush. Satisfied that the makeshift surgery is over, he rejoins us. He crosses himself when he sees the puddle.

"It's Hari's baby," Ira says.

"Should we go?" Hari says.

"That's a baby?" Waynkey says.

I shrug.

"God is close to here," Hari says.

Waynkey leans over the puddle and then jumps back. He seems at a loss of what to do or say. "What should we do?" he says.

"I'm not going with her," Ira says.

I say, "Do what you will. I'm following her."

Waynkey nods. "Do we have an option?"

"So we're following her?" Ira says.

Waynkey and I nod. "It's the only way," he says.

After a pause where she seems to be building up for another shriek, Ira says, "Then I suppose we'd better get on with it."

Hari twirls a finger through the baby puddle. "Night will fall soon. We need to move now," she says, raising the finger to her golden lips to suck away the clown's liquid frown.

CHAPTER FOURTEEN
The Luxury of a Shotgun to the Face

Hari leads us deeper into the blue forest, where goggle-eyed blob creatures eat leaf pods that bleed blue when the translucent blobs bite into them. "These must be ghost embryos," Waynkey says.

"Ghost embryos?" Hari says.

Waynkey nods. "It was written in a very ancient text, more ancient than the Jerry even, about unborn spirits that lived in Paradise Garden long before all other creatures. Most people call it heresy, but I can't say it surprises me that they exist. Most of what we've seen here, I bet a lot of it has been written about. You just have to know where to look."

"Don't listen to half of what he says," I tell Hari.

"They sound like hallucinations," she says.

The farther we walk, the more ghost embryos populate the trees. I regret not starting a map of Paradise Garden at the outset of our journey. At least then future explorers who aren't puppets to the Vatican or the Right Time Consortium would have something to work from.

Hari stops. "God should be right here."

We push through more thickets and our path ends. A gelatinous obsidian monolith taller than any shark we have encountered blocks the way. Robot heads, arms, and other pieces of junk protrude at impossible angles from every side.

"Here he is," Hari says. "Here is your God."

Ira takes two steps back. "I call bullshit, you fucking liar. Look what the robot has done. See where trusting her gets you?"

"No one promised us anything better," I say.

"I can't believe this is fucking God," Ira shrieks, stepping forward and poking me in the chest.

"Yes you can," Waynkey says. He pulls Ira away from me and they bow together in the dirt. "Just bow with me. That's it, just bow. All it takes is faith and worship."

Hari kneels beside them. She must know the whole prayer routine from the Vatican. Ira demon-shrieks as Waynkey tries to appease this holy monstrosity.

Hari looks on in horror, probably mortified by our disparate reactions to God, who could not possibly appear in any form that isn't stupid and absurd because, as I now realize, he exists only in symbiosis with the stupid and absurd.

A hole opens near the top of God's face and gives way to a static, spongy blackness. Three pink urchin-orbs squish out from the inner dark and peer down at us. The skin peels away from the bottom of each urchin and emits a tentacle of light. This light is somehow a visual manifestation of their foil-crinkling voices. In unison, the urchins say, "Bow."

Their tentacle lights wrap around my body. Electric volts blast from their suckers and electrify every hair on my head. My mannequin hand glows chartreuse. Waynkey yanks my robe and pleads for me to bow with them.

"Bow before I Am," say the three pink urchins.

The monolith bends over and folds in half like it's made of peanut butter and honey. It coils up so that the urchins hover directly over us. I shield my eyes so the lights don't blind me. I think of all the UFO abduction reports Wayne used to ramble about. Waynkey paws at my legs as if

97

to rip those memories from my head. "Get down!" he howls.

Stepping away so that he can't hold me back, I raise my glowing hand toward the three urchins and say, "Pow."

Nothing happens at first, then my fingers stretch until they get so thin that through them I spot ghost embryos chomping leaves and flashing me anxious eyes. My mannequin hand pops off at the wrist and floats toward the urchins, the fingers wavering like jellyfish legs. "The jellyfish prophet," they cry. "The jellyfish—"

My hand explodes and showers the urchins in liquid golden particles. I cover my eyes with my remaining hand. The energy from the exploding jellyfish particles knocks me to my knees. The ground sucks at my legs, dragging me beneath the ground. I'm up to my waist before I know it.

Then it all stops. My puppet hand returns and reattaches itself. Everything goes silent. I open my eyes. The monolith has crumpled into a boiling hill of tar.

"Is everybody fine?" I say.

No response. "Is everybody fine?" I repeat.

Waynkey manages to speak between snuffles and hee-haws. "You killed God, you jellyfish prophet," he says. "You killed him and now there's no way for us to know the truth."

Hari stares at the black hill. "Why would you destroy the thing you want most in the universe?" she says.

"My hand did it," I say. "I had nothing to do with it. I didn't choose to be the jellyfish prophet. Is that even a real thing?"

Ira stands and spits a wad of what appears to be light. "If that was God, consider me an atheist," she says.

"Salvation is gone," Waynkey says.

I open my mouth to question if he truly believed salvation would come from three urchin-like saucers who emerged from a gigantic monolith that smelled worse than rancid carp milkshakes, but it isn't any use. He believes I murdered God. After saving their asses, the shame of it all depresses me.

Steam hisses out of God's bubbling corpse. The former monolith lurches forward. The black blob rears back like a horse and three pink balloons float out from its underside. A leprechaun-sized great white shark clutches the string of each balloon. The blob collapses back to the earth. It hardens to the texture of an amphibian and ceases bubbling. The sharks float in figure eight patterns above our heads.

Waynkey falls to his knees again. "My lord, risen from the dead," he says.

The sharks release their balloons and float toward us. "We can forgive you for being born," they say, speaking in unison. "My own birth was an accident, but to intrude on sacred ground like a pack of drunk clowns, that calls for an eternal rot in Hell."

"Good, we're ready to go," Ira says.

"No," Waynkey pleads, "don't listen to her. Don't damn us. We are at your mercy, my lord. We are here to serve you. Is that not what you demand of your children, to be served?"

"I have never demanded anything of you, any of you, and I only do so now because you have ruined Paradise Garden. Your ideals, your odors, the way you dress up in little outfits like paper dolls. Your species is a mistake, a mutation, a disease I wasted billions of years attempting to annihilate. I went to great lengths to fake my own death, and now here you are, poking around my garden and awakening in me the everlasting headache that only vanished several centuries ago. What am I to do? This war inside my head will keep raging until I have removed myself from even the most fragmented memory of you. Unlike you, the universe denies me the luxury of a shotgun to the face, and you spit on it. Rats, vermin . . . scuttle away before the air you breathe mutates me again. Wait, is that a shotgun?"

The three sharks snatch Waynkey's shotgun and juggle it from one to the other. Each shark aims the gun so the barrel jams down its owns throat. One by one, they pull the trigger on themselves and fall to the ground, dead. This is how God kills himself.

Waynkey still hasn't risen from his knees. "This wasn't God, it was Lucifer," he says, but he doesn't sound very sure of himself, all splattered with God's brains.

Ira laughs. She gets a real kick out of God's death. At least we know there isn't much use in putting stock in a decent afterlife. Maybe that's something worth laughing over. I don't know. Right now, I have no fucking clue how I feel about God telling us to fuck off and stay fucked off. Until recently, I can't say precisely when, meeting God would have been the greatest thing ever. I wonder what changed, what makes me sad and drugged-feeling about the God sharks committing suicide. Maybe it's because I'm the jellyfish prophet, whatever that means.

Mechanical shouts rise from the other side of the tar hill and disturb us from our stupor. Hari springs alert and wraps her arms around my neck. "It must be Sadhara," she says.

I lift my puppet hand and point at the black mass that had once been part of God. "What do you expect me to do? God over there, that's who we always cried to in desperate times. Just look at him now. What's left?"

"That is a man?" Hari says, her circuits probably going haywire.

Before I can explain anything, a glop of sludge splatters across my face. I rub a sleeve over my mouth, struggling to get the burning acid taste off my tongue,

The tin-hollow voice of Sadhara: "Surrender."

I clear the muck from my eyes enough to see the robot chief standing atop the mountain of God. One robot stands at his left and another at his right, but it doesn't appear that any of them are responsible for tossing the black muck. Waynkey points to a far corner of the hill and says, "Something's happening."

Sure enough, a few bubbles sputter in the air before floating away. One of them crashes down off to our right. Sadhara, unaware of the slime balls, demands that we surrender to his indomitable will. "Surrender humans," he says. "Hari, seize the enemy and return to your master."

The bubbles spread around the base of the black hill and work their way up. Before they reach the robots and before the robots notice, the body of God morphs into a massive white egg. Sadhara and the other robots, unprepared for the instant transformation, lose their balance and slip the sixty-plus feet to the ground. Sadhara hits the blue forest soil and backflips to his feet. The other two robots remain state of the art junk piles.

Sadhara stands poised in a bizarre martial arts stance and waves his fingers for us to approach.

"What do we do?" Waynkey says.

Hari pulls me close to her, her breathe hot against my neck. "Sadhara is the greatest martial artist in the universe. He rarely enters Satchitananda because his power is so grand that he risks defeating himself. Even your puppet power will be useless against him," she says.

"Satchi-what?" I ask.

"It is the final stage of liberation. You might think

of Satchitananda as physical enlightenment. He is the only martial artist to have ever reached it."

"Did you hear that?" I say to Waynkey and Ira.

"She knew this all along and didn't tell us?" Ira says, sliding a razor-edged page from her Jerry.

I try loosening Hari's stranglehold on me. "So he's a sort of priest like us except that he's a robot and kicks way more ass?"

She shakes her head. "Not just a priest. He is everything."

We shift our frightened, half-wild gazes toward Sadhara to get a look at this enlightened ass-kicker. He remains dormant except for the waving fingers. He shouts, "Are you coming or not?"

Ghost embryos crowd around us. They twitter squeaky circus noises that may or may not signify curiosity. Despite crowding close to our side of the clearing, they steer clear of Sadhara and the massive egg. When one of them is pushed closer to the egg than it wants to be, it squeals.

The egg trembles and splits down the middle. All the ghost embryos scream together and it occurs to me that they may as well be angels.

Sadhara seizes advantage of the embryo stampede and charges. I try to smile at this superman who will tear through us like a gymnast made of ninja stars. I take a deep breath and raise my puppet hand. The others look on in terror but make no move to stop me. If they have no better plan, what does it matter anyway?

Sadhara blazes past us and then twirls around to stand toe to toe with Waynkey. I dive for the robot, hoping to catch him off guard. With an effortless sidestep, Sadhara knocks me to the ground. "Help! Get him off!" I cry, but even Hari stands rigid and helpless.

The robot slugs me in the gut hard enough that I puke in his face. I flail my arms but find nothing to grasp, nowhere to go. He wipes away the vomit and punches me in the face. He uncoils his fist, revealing five fingers sheathed in shark teeth. Laughing feverishly, he digs the toothed fingers into my gut and twitters them around.

Sadhara plucks his fingers out of my ruined flesh and turns to face the others. I struggle against blacking out. If I do, I know my body will give it all up and the others will die as well. You can regret something and still hold it more sacred than anything else, and at the very least I have to stay alive for them. Breathing in and out in rapid succession, I tucked my guts back where they belong.

Sadhara buzzes at Hari. They must be arguing. I crawl toward them half inch by half inch. My head feels like a concrete block with two holes drilled in it for eyes.

I reach out and brush a hazy figure as it dashes by. I shut my eyes and rub them until color spots appear. Then I open them again. The figure that slipped by me blocks my path.

Waynkey. He stands pure and rigid, a mannequin. He will never return from the private booth inside his porcelain head. Their head. No use denying the dual nature there. I stare at my palms, at my eviscerated torso.

Ira hyperventilates. "How could you?" she says.

The event must fuck with Hari's programming. She seems to have forgotten all about Sadhara and stares at Waynkey, the newest addition to my world of mannequins. I open my mouth to apologize but fail to form the right words. In the end there's never much to say but a sheepish apology.

His eyes remain open, and despite being made of porcelain and despite him not being there anymore, the

103

essence of both Wayne and Donkey emanates from those eyes. I force myself to look away. He reminds me of ancient Greek statues and in my condition I can't bear imagining someone I know staring on through the centuries like that.

Hari and Ira kneel beside me. They speak, but their words enter my skull as fuzz. Their voices warm a hollow place in my belly. Where's Sadhara? In the corner of my tunnel vision, I glimpse a shape darting toward the gargantuan egg, which has very nearly split in two. And then a voice does reach me. I'm uncertain whether it's Hari or Ira who says it, but whoever it is says, "Everything is going to be fine."

Chapter Fifteen
PAPER GARDEN

I cough up blood as they drag me away from Sadhara and the giant egg. Hari and Ira drop me in a pile of swamp muck beneath a drooping blue tree. Landing on my back, I stare up at them and apologize for bleeding everywhere. No words come out, just blood that chunks up the more it flows. Hari licks my blood off her lips with her golden robot tongue. Ira crouches and wipes the blood from my eyes. "Can you see better?" she asks.

Nodding, I strain my neck to get a view of the giant egg. Although Hari and Ira block most of it from my line of vision, I spot something else, something rising from the eggshell.

Two clawed arms, each larger than any shark we have encountered, bursts into the air. The head of the hatching god-creature rises from the broken shell. Its blue, bone-like flesh shimmers. The god-creature towers above Sadhara, blocking out the green sky. Spidery blue veins pulse in its arms and legs, limbs bigger than cruise ships. It takes a step and the ground quakes.

I cough dark blood. Nausea sits on my chest and squeezes the air from my lungs. I puke down my chest. Hari and Ira don't notice. They shake their heads as if a little denial is all it takes to make a mega-shark disappear. We're too far away to gauge Sadhara's expression, but he must

105

realize he's met his match.

The robot poses in karate stance and charges one of the mega-shark's fin-shaped feet. The robot chops at the shark's foot. Hari gasps.

The mega-shark, still swinging its arms, grins at Sadhara. The robot gapes up at the creature and then down at the arm he struck with, which was neatly severed during his own assault.

"This won't last much longer," Ira says.

"We have nowhere to go," Hari says.

They stare at me and I pray to God they aren't about to abandon me for shark food. The mega-shark raises the foot Sadhara struck and attempts to stomp on the robot. Sadhara barrel rolls away just in time, but the tremors from the impact splay him on his back. Ghost embryos tumble from trees, squealing and tittering for new shelter.

Sadhara reaches both arms behind his neck and booms out a command. His bent arms jut out and grow. They expand outward to form a set of wings spanning ten feet. He leaps into the air, flapping away from the mega-shark . . . flying directly toward us.

"We've got to go," Ira screams. She tugs at my arm but my body is only so much dead weight.

Hari pushes her away. Ira demon-shrieks, too petrified to take any sort of action. Hari wipes the blood and puke from my mouth. She lowers her face to mine. She doesn't actually kiss me, just lets her cold metal lips rest against mine. I'm too weak and bewildered to resist. She pulls away and says, "Now I want you to transform yourself into a mannequin."

"What do you mean?" I say, my eyes glazing over.

Sheets of green and black paper flutter down as the mega-shark rips a hole in the sky. A stream of sharks pours in from the hole.

Sadhara spins around in the air. He looks directly at us and shakes his head, as if troubled over who he wants to kill more: us or the sharks.

"Become a mannequin," Hari says.

"Tell me why," I say.

Again, she presses her lips against mine.

Sadhara's hesitation forces him to stand off against the sharks, who now fill every corner of the crumbling sky not occupied by the mega-shark. Despite having only one arm, a single touch from Sadhara's remaining hand destroys a dozen sharks at once, sending them flopping to the earth like canned sardines.

Ira is still pissed about Hari pushing her. How she manages to sulk about getting pushed when we stand right at the edge of the world, where the shark son of God destroys the only remaining fragment of our collective dream, is beyond me. Maybe that isn't her problem at all. I never know with her. Everything below my neck goes numb and it gets harder and harder not to shut my eyes for good.

The sharks overwhelm Sadhara. A baby shark nips at his foot, distracting him long enough for a thirty-footer to munch away his legs. His wings go next, as if they're fragile as butterfly wings, and then the entire army of sharks rushes him from every direction, frenziedly gnashing and mixing their shark blood with machine blood.

I think about formulating my last rites. Then it hits me that nothing remains of God but a mutated shark tearing down the old sky to make room for a sky of sharks.

Hari and Ira huddle beside me. They stare in bug-eyed terror as Paradise Garden flakes away in the jaws of sharks. What the hell, if there won't be any afterlife, will claiming one final casualty really hurt my future prospects? I open my mouth to thank Hari and Ira for everything they've done for me. I gargle blood and exhale a last gasp that neither of them notice. Turning my so-called blessing against myself, I close my eyes and envision myself a mannequin, wandering a garden with all the mannequins I have ever forsaken.

CHAPTER SIXTEEN
Internal Gravity

I'm hanging from a tree branch. For years I always told myself that hanging would be my method of suicide if it ever came to that. Now I worry that it has. My guts ache like a Horseman of the Apocalypse Hangover. A white rubber chord juts from my bellybutton and splits in two directions. One side of the tube ends at Ira's bellybutton. The other juts out of Hari's mouth and resembles a giant straw. I rub my eyes with porcelain hands and look around. Scrap mechanical parts suspend us from the tree branch. All of it, however, is white. Not just the tree or the mechanical parts, but every tree that I can see and also the ground, the sky, and even Hari and Ira. Towering far above it all, the shark son of God stretches his skyscraper arms into the porcelain sky as if to hold it all up, which he may very well be doing.

Only in the shadows cast down by some invisible light can anything be discerned from anything else. Inspecting our tree more closely, it strikes me how much the tree resembles a deformed cricket.

The branches of the Tree of Knowledge twitch and tremble. The mechanical parts restraining me break away. As for Hari and Ira, they have yet to speak or show any sign of life. Dead maybe, or just two more for my collection. The idea nauseates me even more than the slug-swirling chaos in my gut.

From our place at the top of the tree, the three of us tumble to the bottom. The bodies of Hari and Ira *egg-crack!* upon impact. Instantly, they spring to their feet.

"You're a toad," Ira says, "and I'm a manne—"

"Is this still the past?" Hari interrupts.

Examining my body, I realize that Ira is right. Or partially so. My face feels the same, but my legs are the toad form of me.

Scratching my head, I say, "So what do we do now that death isn't—"

Hari throws her arms around my neck, choking me. "We can be Adam and Eve," she says. "It would be very sad to go on in these new bodies and pretend nothing is wrong. Adam and Eve sound like very nice people to be."

"There are three of us," Ira says. I recall what she said about fighting Hari. "And you can't just choose to be Adam and Eve. Didn't the Vatican program anything into that head of yours?"

Hari nuzzles into my chest. "We can be Adam and Eve," she whispers, "we can be anyone we want."

I close my eyes to hide from the dizzy whirl of whiteness but it's the same inside my head, as if my mind has been replaced by a slab of consciousness outside time, beyond cobwebs. "It would be good to be Adam and Eve," I smile. And why not?

"I'll repeat myself," Ira says, "there are *three* of us."

"But Adam and Eve never existed in Paradise Garden, and we are all attached. We will find a new garden," Hari says.

I hold her closer. "Which means we can be anything we want. Look around us, Ira, and tell me why we aren't free to—"

Crack! Lightning pain destroys my skull.

Then vanishes. I blink, doubled over and gripping my side, afraid the pain might return. The object that hit me on the head lays at my feet. My vision blurry, I pick it up. It is a key.

"A key to unlock our new garden?" Hari says.

Ira scoffs. "How should he know?"

Holding the tooth-like key in my hand, I eye the two mannequins standing before me. This mannequin world blossomed around us so suddenly that only now do I recall the blood I lost in the former Paradise. I swallow the notion that all this might be nothing more than death. For all I know, we could have died back on the Gib . . . the name escapes me.

"What is it?" Hari says.

I gaze off beyond them. A black rectangle stands at the base of the Tree of Knowledge. Apparently it's part of the trunk. I squint against all the whiteness and distinguish a tiny white dot on one side of the dark shape. The rectangle must be a door.

I stumble over mannequin leaves toward the Tree of Knowledge. I run as fast as my awkward legs allow. The white chord connecting all of us forces Hari and Ira to dash after me.

I crouch and try catching a glimpse through the door's keyhole. No luck.

"What do you see?" Hari says.

"Can't see a thing," I say, still hoping to get a peek at something. I raise the key to the lock. "The key will fit, though."

Ira sighs and says, "Is a door that goddamn special? We're all mannequins for shit's sake."

"Being this way feels almost normal," Hari says.

"You've got robot experience," Ira says, but then she laughs, real bright and beautiful, as if she's suddenly been lifted out of herself. "I guess you're right. It's not much different, in a strange way . . . less internal gravity."

"So we open the door?" I say, raising the key. Given time to think it over, Ira might change her mind on this one.

"So we become Adam and Eve?" Hari says.

"No," Ira says. "There's one last thing to do." She strips from her porcelain robe and bends over to take off her boots. She smiles up at me and says, "We shouldn't be needing these."

I hand the key to Hari and remove my own boots and robe, so glad and sick and afraid because I am new again, or almost new. We're not quite there yet. We stand naked and not at all ashamed. Hari inserts the key into its hole. "Everything will be fine," she says, and suddenly my heart aches for reasons I don't understand, but I am okay with that. Sometimes that ache is all you've got to work with, and you can still make everything fine in the end. You can still make it if you try.

ABOUT THE AUTHOR

Cameron Pierce has been a loyal supporter of the bizarro fiction movement since he was a teenager. Over the years, Cameron has slowly become more involved in the bizarro scene and now as an author he has become the newest member of the bizarro family with his first novel, *Shark Hunting in Paradise Garden*. His fiction and poetry has appeared in *Bust Down the Door and Eat All the Chickens*, *The Dream People*, *Bare Bone*, *The Horror Library Vol. II*, *Sein und Werden*, and *Avant-Garde for the New Millenium*. He lives in Olympia, WA.

For free and easy loan quotes, visit him online at www. deadamericanchildren.com.

ABOUT THE ARTIST

Bernard Dumaine is a French artist most well known for his works in the surrealism and photorealism styles and for his background designs for television cartoons. He works in a variety of media, including oil paints, acrylic paints, graphite pencil, digital painting, digital collage, and video.

Bizarro books

CATALOG FALL 2008

Bizarro Books publishes under the following imprints:

RAW DOG SCREAMING PRESS

www.rawdogscreamingpress.com

www.eraserheadpress.com

AFTERBIRTH BOOKS

www.afterbirthbooks.com

Swallowdown

Press

www.swallowdownpress.com

For all your Bizarro needs visit:

WWW.BIZARROCENTRAL.COM

Introduce yourselves to the bizarro genre and all of its authors with the Bizarro Starter Kit series. Each volume features short novels and short stories by ten of the leading bizarro authors, designed to give you a perfect sampling of the genre for only $5 plus shipping.

BB-0X1
"The Bizarro Starter Kit"
(Orange)

Featuring D. Harlan Wilson, Carlton Mellick III, Jeremy Robert Johnson, Kevin L Donihe, Gina Ranalli, Andre Duza, Vincent W. Sakowski, Steve Beard, John Edward Lawson, and Bruce Taylor.

236 pages $5

BB-0X2
"The Bizarro Starter Kit"
(Blue)

Featuring Ray Fracalossy, Jeremy C. Shipp, Jordan Krall, Mykle Hansen, Andersen Prunty, Eckhard Gerdes, Bradley Sands, Steve Aylett, Christian TeBordo, and Tony Rauch.

244 pages $5

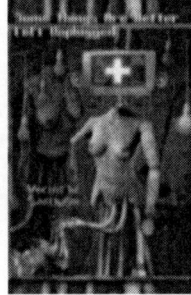

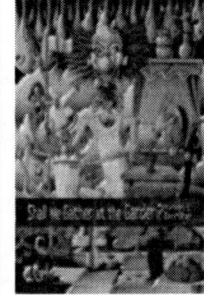

BB-001 **"The Kafka Effekt" D. Harlan Wilson** - A collection of forty-four irreal short stories loosely written in the vein of Franz Kafka, with more than a pinch of William S. Burroughs sprinkled on top. **211 pages $14**

BB-002 **"Satan Burger" Carlton Mellick III** - The cult novel that put Carlton Mellick III on the map ... Six punks get jobs at a fast food restaurant owned by the devil in a city violently overpopulated by surreal alien cultures. **236 pages $14**

BB-003 **"Some Things Are Better Left Unplugged" Vincent Sakwoski** - Join The Man and his Nemesis, the obese tabby, for a nightmare roller coaster ride into this postmodern fantasy. **152 pages $10**

BB-004 **"Shall We Gather At the Garden?" Kevin L Donihe** - Donihe's Debut novel. Midgets take over the world, The Church of Lionel Richie vs. The Church of the Byrds, plant porn and more! **244 pages $14**

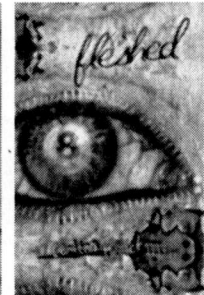

BB-005 **"Razor Wire Pubic Hair" Carlton Mellick III** - A genderless humandildo is purchased by a razor dominatrix and brought into her nightmarish world of bizarre sex and mutilation. **176 pages $11**

BB-006 **"Stranger on the Loose" D. Harlan Wilson** - The fiction of Wilson's 2nd collection is planted in the soil of normalcy, but what grows out of that soil is a dark, witty, otherworldly jungle... **228 pages $14**

BB-007 **"The Baby Jesus Butt Plug" Carlton Mellick III** - Using clones of the Baby Jesus for anal sex will be the hip sex fetish of the future. **92 pages $10**

BB-008 **"Fishyfleshed" Carlton Mellick III** - The world of the past is an illogical flatland lacking in dimension and color, a sick-scape of crispy squid people wandering the desert for no apparent reason. **260 pages $14**

BB-009 **"Dead Bitch Army" Andre Duza** - Step into a world filled with racist teenagers, cannibals, 100 warped Uncle Sams, automobiles with razor-sharp teeth, living graffiti, and a pissed-off zombie bitch out for revenge. **344 pages $16**

BB-010 **"The Menstruating Mall" Carlton Mellick III** - "The Breakfast Club meets Chopping Mall as directed by David Lynch." - Brian Keene **212 pages $12**

BB-011 **"Angel Dust Apocalypse" Jeremy Robert Johnson** - Methheads, man-made monsters, and murderous Neo-Nazis. "Seriously amazing short stories..." - Chuck Palahniuk, author of Fight Club **184 pages $11**

BB-012 **"Ocean of Lard" Kevin L Donihe / Carlton Mellick III** - A parody of those old Choose Your Own Adventure kid's books about some very odd pirates sailing on a sea made of animal fat. **176 pages $12**

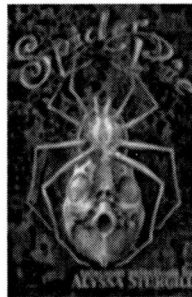

BB-013 **"Last Burn in Hell" John Edward Lawson** - From his lurid angstaffair with a lesbian music diva to his ascendance as unlikely pop icon the one constant for Kenrick Brimley, official state prison gigolo, is he's got no clue what he's doing. **172 pages $14**

BB-014 **"Tangerinephant" Kevin Dole 2** - TV-obsessed aliens have abducted Michael Tangerinephant in this bizarro combination of science fiction, satire, and surrealism. **164 pages $11**

BB-015 **"Foop!" Chris Genoa** - Strange happenings are going on at Dactyl, Inc, the world's first and only time travel tourism company. "A surreal pie in the face!" - Christopher Moore **300 pages $14**

BB-016 **"Spider Pie" Alyssa Sturgill** - A one-way trip down a rabbit hole inhabited by sexual deviants and friendly monsters, fairytale beginnings and hideous endings. **104 pages $11**

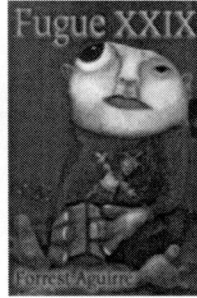

BB-017 "The Unauthorized Woman" Efrem Emerson - Enter the world of the inner freak, a landscape populated by the pre-dead and morticioners, by cockroaches and 300-lb robots. **104 pages $11**

BB-018 "Fugue XXIX" Forrest Aguirre - Tales from the fringe of speculative literary fiction where innovative minds dream up the future's uncharted territories while mining forgotten treasures of the past. **220 pages $16**

BB-019 "Pocket Full of Loose Razorblades" John Edward Lawson - A collection of dark bizarro stories. From a giant rectum to a foot-fungus factory to a girl with a biforked tongue. **190 pages $13**

BB-020 "Punk Land" Carlton Mellick III - In the punk version of Heaven, the anarchist utopia is threatened by corporate fascism and only Goblin, Mortician's sperm, and a blue-mohawked female assassin named Shark Girl can stop them. **284 pages $15**

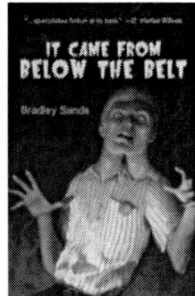

BB-021"Pseudo-City" D. Harlan Wilson - Pseudo-City exposes what waits in the bathroom stall, under the manhole cover and in the corporate boardroom, all in a way that can only be described as mind-bogglingly irreal. **220 pages $16**

BB-022 "Kafka's Uncle and Other Strange Tales" Bruce Taylor - Anslenot and his giant tarantula (tormentor? fri-end?) wander a desecrated world in this novel and collection of stories from Mr. Magic Realism Himself. **348 pages $17**

BB-023 "Sex and Death In Television Town" Carlton Mellick III - In the old west, a gang of hermaphrodite gunslingers take refuge from a demon plague in Telos: a town where its citizens have televisions instead of heads. **184 pages $12**

BB-024 "It Came From Below The Belt" Bradley Sands - What can Grover Goldstein do when his severed, sentient penis forces him to return to high school and help it win the presidential election? **204 pages $13**

BB-025 **"Sick: An Anthology of Illness" John Lawson, editor** - These Sick stories are horrendous and hilarious dissections of creative minds on the scalpel's edge. **296 pages $16**

BB-026 **"Tempting Disaster" John Lawson, editor** - A shocking and alluring anthology from the fringe that examines our culture's obsession with taboos. **260 pages $16**

BB-027 **"Siren Promised" Jeremy Robert Johnson** - Nominated for the Bram Stoker Award. A potent mix of bad drugs, bad dreams, brutal bad guys, and surreal/incredible art by Alan M. Clark. **190 pages $13**

BB-028 **"Chemical Gardens" Gina Ranalli** - Ro and punk band Green is the Enemy find Kreepkins, a surfer-dude warlock, a vengeful demon, and a Metal Priestess in their way as they try to escape an underground nightmare. **188 pages $13**

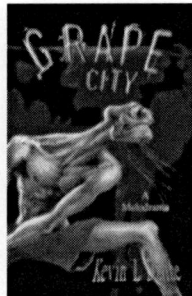

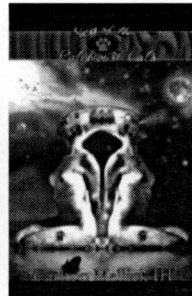

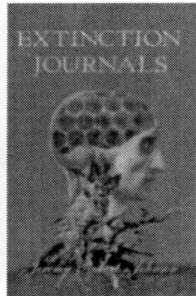

BB-029 **"Jesus Freaks" Andre Duza** - For God so loved the world that he gave his only two begotten sons... and a few million zombies. **400 pages $16**

BB-030 **"Grape City" Kevin L. Donihe** - More Donihe-style comedic bizarro about a demon named Charles who is forced to work a minimum wage job on Earth after Hell goes out of business. **108 pages $10**

BB-031**"Sea of the Patchwork Cats" Carlton Mellick III** - A quiet dreamlike tale set in the ashes of the human race. For Mellick enthusiasts who also adore The Twilight Zone. **112 pages $10**

BB-032 **"Extinction Journals" Jeremy Robert Johnson** - An uncanny voyage across a newly nuclear America where one man must confront the problems associated with loneliness, insane dieties, radiation, love, and an ever-evolving cockroach suit with a mind of its own. **104 pages $10**

BB-033 "Meat Puppet Cabaret" Steve Beard - At last! The secret connection between Jack the Ripper and Princess Diana's death revealed! **240 pages $16 / $30**

BB-034 "The Greatest Fucking Moment in Sports" Kevin L. Donihe - In the tradition of the surreal anti-sitcom Get A Life comes a tale of triumph and agape love from the master of comedic bizarro. **108 pages $10**

BB-035 "The Troublesome Amputee" John Edward Lawson - Disturbing verse from a man who truly believes nothing is sacred and intends to prove it. **104 pages $9**

BB-036 "Deity" Vic Mudd - God (who doesn't like to be called "God") comes down to a typical, suburban, Ohio family for a little vacation—but it doesn't turn out to be as relaxing as He had hoped it would be... **168 pages $12**

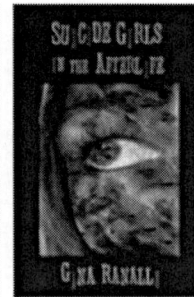

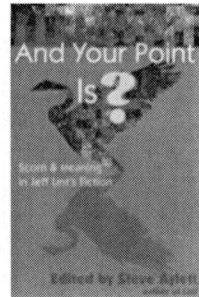

BB-037 "The Haunted Vagina" Carlton Mellick III - It's difficult to love a woman whose vagina is a gateway to the world of the dead. **132 pages $10**

BB-038 "Tales from the Vinegar Wasteland" Ray Fracalossy - Witness: a man is slowly losing his face, a neighbor who periodically screams out for no apparent reason, and a house with a room that doesn't actually exist. **240 pages $14**

BB-039 "Suicide Girls in the Afterlife" Gina Ranalli - After Pogue commits suicide, she unexpectedly finds herself an unwilling "guest" at a hotel in the Afterlife, where she meets a group of bizarre characters, including a goth Satan, a hippie Jesus, and an alien-human hybrid. **100 pages $9**

BB-040 "And Your Point Is?" Steve Aylett - In this follow-up to LINT multiple authors provide critical commentary and essays about Jeff Lint's mind-bending literature. **104 pages $11**

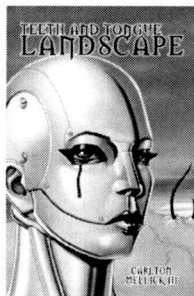

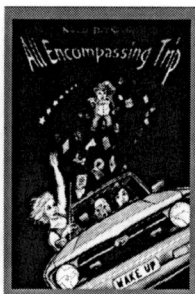

BB-041 "Not Quite One of the Boys" Vincent Sakowski - While drug-dealer Maxi drinks with Dante in purgatory, God and Satan play a little tri-level chess and do a little bargaining over his business partner, Vinnie, who is still left on earth. **220 pages $14**

BB-042 "Teeth and Tongue Landscape" Carlton Mellick III - On a planet made out of meat, a socially-obsessive monophobic man tries to find his place amongst the strange creatures and communities that he comes across. **110 pages $10**

BB-043 "War Slut" Carlton Mellick III - Part "1984," part "Waiting for Godot," and part action horror video game adaptation of John Carpenter's "The Thing." **116 pages $10**

BB-044 "All Encompassing Trip" Nicole Del Sesto - In a world where coffee is no longer available, the only television shows are reality TV re-runs, and the animals are talking back, Nikki, Amber and a singing Coyote in a do-rag are out to restore the light **308 pages $15**

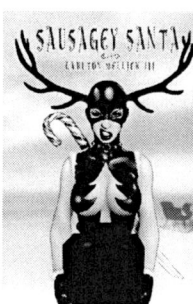

BB-045 "Dr. Identity" D. Harlan Wilson - Follow the Dystopian Duo on a killing spree of epic proportions through the irreal postcapitalist city of Bliptown where time ticks sideways, artificial Bug-Eyed Monsters punish citizens for consumer-capitalist lethargy, and ultraviolence is as essential as a daily multivitamin. **208 pages $15**

BB-046 "The Million-Year Centipede" Eckhard Gerdes - Wakelin, frontman for 'The Hinge,' wrote a poem so prophetic that to ignore it dooms a person to drown in blood. **130 pages $12**

BB-047 "Sausagey Santa" Carlton Mellick III - A bizarro Christmas tale featuring Santa as a piratey mutant with a body made of sausages. 124 pages $10

BB-048 "Misadventures in a Thumbnail Universe" Vincent Sakowski - Dive deep into the surreal and satirical realms of neo-classical Blender Fiction, filled with television shoes and flesh-filled skies. **120 pages $10**

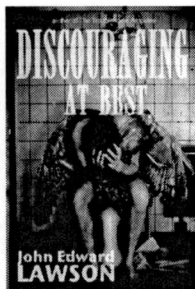

BB-049 **"Vacation" Jeremy C. Shipp** - Blueblood Bernard Johnson leaved his boring life behind to go on The Vacation, a year-long corporate sponsored odyssey. But instead of seeing the world, Bernard is captured by terrorists, becomes a key figure in secret drug wars, and, worse, doesn't once miss his secure American Dream. **160 pages $14**

BB-051 **"13 Thorns" Gina Ranalli** - Thirteen tales of twisted, bizarro horror. **240 pages $13**

BB-050 **"Discouraging at Best" John Edward Lawson** - A collection where the absurdity of the mundane expands exponentially creating a tidal wave that sweeps reason away. For those who enjoy satire, bizarro, or a good old-fashioned slap to the senses. **208 pages $15**

BB-052 **"Better Ways of Being Dead" Christian TeBordo** - In this class, the students have to keep one palm down on the table at all times, and listen to lectures about a panda who speaks Chinese. **216 pages $14**

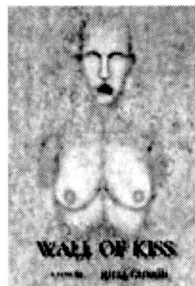

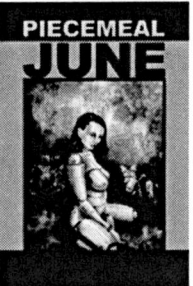

BB-053 **"Ballad of a Slow Poisoner" Andrew Goldfarb** Millford Mutterwurst sat down on a Tuesday to take his afternoon tea, and made the unpleasant discovery that his elbows were becoming flatter. **128 pages $10**

BB-054 **"Wall of Kiss" Gina Ranalli** - A woman... A wall... Sometimes love blooms in the strangest of places. **108 pages $9**

BB-055 **"HELP! A Bear is Eating Me" Mykle Hansen** - The bizarro, heartwarming, magical tale of poor planning, hubris and severe blood loss... **150 pages $11**

BB-056 **"Piecemeal June" Jordan Krall** - A man falls in love with a living sex doll, but with love comes danger when her creator comes after her with crab-squid assassins. **90 pages $9**

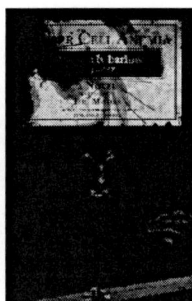

BB-057 "Laredo" Tony Rauch - Dreamlike, surreal stories by Tony Rauch. 180 pages $12

BB-058 "The Overwhelming Urge" Andersen Prunty - A collection of bizarro tales by Andersen Prunty. 150 pages $11

BB-059 "Adolf in Wonderland" Carlton Mellick III - A dreamlike adventure that takes a young descendant of Adolf Hitler's design and sends him down the rabbit hole into a world of imperfection and disorder. 180 pages $11

BB-060 "Super Cell Anemia" Duncan B. Barlow - "Unrelentingly bizarre and mysterious, unsettling in all the right ways..." - Brian Evenson. 180 pages $12

BB-061 "Ultra Fuckers" Carlton Mellick III - Absurdist suburban horror about a couple who enter an upper middle class gated community but can't find their way out. 108 pages $9

BB-062 "House of Houses" Kevin L. Donihe - An odd man wants to marry his house. Unfortunately, all of the houses in the world collapse at the same time in the Great House Holocaust. Now he must travel to House Heaven to find his departed fiancee. 172 pages $11

BB-063 "Necro Sex Machine" Andre Duza - The Dead Bicth returns in this follow-up to the bizarro zombie epic Dead Bitch Army. 400 pages $16

BB-064 "Squid Pulp Blues" Jordan Krall - In these three bizarro-noir novellas, the reader is thrown into a world of murderers, drugs made from squid parts, deformed gun-toting veterans, and a mischievous apocalyptic donkey. 204 pages $12

BB-065 "Jack and Mr. Grin" Andersen Prunty - "When Mr. Grin calls you can hear a smile in his voice. Not a warm and friendly smile, but the kind that seizes your spine in fear. You don't need to pay your phone bill to hear it. That smile is in every line of Prunty's prose." - Tom Bradley. **208 pages $12**

BB-066 "Cybernetrix" Carlton Mellick III - What would you do if your normal everyday world was slowly mutating into the video game world from Tron? **212 pages $12**

BB-067 "Lemur" Tom Bradley - Spencer Sproul is a would-be serial-killing bus boy who can't manage to murder, injure, or even scare anybody. However, there are other ways to do damage to far more people and do it legally... **120 pages $12**

BB-068 "Cocoon of Terror" Jason Earls - Decapitated corpses...a sculpture of terror...Zelian's masterpiece, his Cocoon of Terror, will trigger a supernatural disaster for everyone on Earth. **196 pages $14**

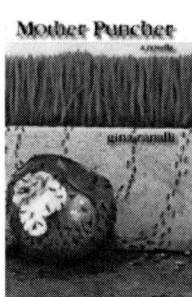

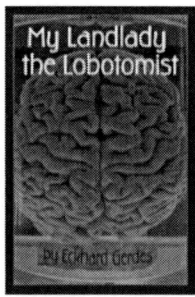

BB-069 "Mother Puncher" Gina Ranalli - The world has become tragically over-populated and now the government strongly opposes procreation. Ed is employed by the government as a mother-puncher. He doesn't relish his job, but he knows it has to be done and he knows he's the best one to do it. **120 pages $9**

BB-070 "My Landlady the Lobotomist" Eckhard Gerdes - The brains of past tenants line the shelves of my boarding house, soaking in a mysterious elixir. One more slip-up and the landlady might just add my frontal lobe to her collection. **116 pages $12**

BB-071 "CPR for Dummies" Mickey Z. - This hilarious freakshow at the world's end is the fragmented, sobering debut novel by acclaimed nonfiction author Mickey Z. **216 pages $14**

BB-072 "Zerostrata" Andersen Prunty - Hansel Nothing lives in a tree house, suffers from memory loss, has a very eccentric family, and falls in love with a woman who runs naked through the woods every night. **144 pages $11**

ORDER FORM

TITLES	QTY	PRICE	TOTAL

Please make checks and moneyorders payable to ROSE O'KEEFE / BIZARRO BOOKS in U.S. funds only. Please don't send bad checks! Allow 2-6 weeks for delivery. International orders may take longer. If you'd like to pay online via PAYPAL.COM, send payments to publisher@eraserheadpress.com.

SHIPPING: US ORDERS - $2 for the first book, $1 for each additional book. For priority shipping, add an additional $4. INT'L ORDERS - $5 for the first book, $3 for each additional book. Add an additional $5 per book for global priority shipping.

Send payment to:

BIZARRO BOOKS
  C/O Rose O'Keefe
  205 NE Bryant
  Portland, OR 97211

Address

City   State   Zip

Email   Phone

Lightning Source UK Ltd.
Milton Keynes UK
UKOW031937130513

210602UK00020B/1569/P